H K FINLEY

The
WORTHY
Cause

ISBN: 061595300X
ISBN 13: 9780615953007
Library of Congress Control Number: 2014902537
Hannah K. Finley, Cincinnati, OH

The Worthy Cause is a work of fiction. Names, characters, places, and incidents are either the product of the author's imagination or are used fictitiously. Any resemblence to actual persons, living or dead, events, or places is entirely coincidental.

Contents

Chapter 1

Delphi Pond - Sabbath Dyme - May 18, 2013 - 9:00 p.m.

S abbath Dyme stared in detached fascination as his wife, Dawn, fell backward over the rail. As he watched, she vanished, disappeared as if she had never existed. Her fall from the deck was as silent as an owl's flight, not even the sound of a splash came from the darkness. Sabbath suddenly remembered that Connie Horton's fraternal grandmother's cremated bones were in that pond. He wondered why he had recalled that now and was momentarily distracted by the jumble of unconnected thoughts rushing through his head. Then one word flashed into his mind, spurring him into action. *Dawn.* Dyme rushed down the stairs two at a time, trying to get to the water as quickly as he could. Dawn gone? How was that possible? What had he done? He found the flashlight Connie kept above the door of the ground floor room and dashed outside where he systematically searched the water, frantically calling her name. Nothing. He'd heard the story about that preacher getting caught on underwater branches and drowning. That was sixty years ago. Could trees underwater stay intact that long? Sabbath didn't know much about trees; he'd spent half of his thirty-six years in prison.

Dyme waded in up to his waist and noticed for the first time how fast the water was moving toward the spillway. Maybe Dawn had gone over the back of it. He wasn't sure that could happen so quickly but he was desperate to find his wife. He screamed out into the night, screamed at his ignorance, his wasted life.

Dyme struggled to shore and then followed the moving water to the spillway. Water. Water—his enemy. He didn't know if the flow was strong enough to carry away a woman Dawn's size. He didn't even know if she could swim. So he walked the creek that was formed by the water that flowed over the spillway. The creek followed the contour of the woods behind the house. Dyme called her name, hoping to find her alive. He didn't know any more about nature than he did about women. As he searched, he remembered the first night they were together after that big party at the fancy hotel in Memphis. The night of his release. He had hesitated before getting into the bed beside her. She'd said, "Don't worry about sex with me. If it's meant to happen, it will. It may take some time." Dawn didn't judge. She was patient and comforting.

Dyme had been relieved she didn't ask about prison and what went on there, before he was put on death row, so that eventually he needed surgery just to take a crap. Death row had felt like a sanctuary. Dyme didn't know the comfort of snuggling with a woman and falling to sleep with her next to him. All of his sexual experience had been in the back of a car, or the woods, never in a bed. Dawn had gotten out of bed, pulled the cushions off the sleeper sofa, and popped up the mattress. She pulled the mattress off its frame and put the foam on the floor. "Does this look more like home?"

He didn't answer.

"Sabbath, it's your choice. You're free to make your own decisions now." Dyme chose the floor. Over the next year plus of travel, that's the way they'd slept and it had worked for them.

How could he betray a woman so kind? He grew more panicked as he looked for Dawn. Dawn was always with him, how could she be gone now? He was thinking these thoughts when he felt something hard jab him in the lower back. Force of habit, he froze.

"Lookin' for somethin', fella?"

Dyme slowly turned to see a big man wearing a camo mask, the whole camo hunting costume, pointing a gun at him. He focused on the outfit not the gun. "Is it hunting season?"

"Yeah. I'm a hunter."

"Please. I need help. My wife fell off the deck into the water. I'm trying to find her. She may have hit her head. She may be wandering around hurt." Dyme had no idea who was accosting him in full deer stalking gear.

"You're real stupid if you think she would be in the creek after a fall off that deck."

"I looked for her in the water. Maybe she sank. Maybe a tree snagged her and is holding her under. Alligators. Are there alligators in the pond or are they just in Florida? I heard this used to be a swamp. Aren't alligators in swamps?" Dyme rambled. He'd lost complete control of his thoughts.

"Fella, I think you better walk back the way you came." The hunter indicated the direction with his gun.

Now Dyme focused on the gun. "What are you doing with that?" Dyme knew less about guns than he did about women and nature. His eyes fell to the big man's left hand. He was holding Dawn's computer case.

"Thank god. That's my wife's. Give it to me." Dyme reached for the case.

The hunter struck him hard on the side of the head with the revolver. Dyme fell in the creek, unconscious. The other man turned Dyme faceup and dragged him to Connie's storage shed like he was a sack of garbage, and to the hunter that was exactly what Dyme was, garbage.

From somewhere in his stupor, Sabbath Dyme heard the door slam shut. Relief. This charade of freedom was over. He was a prisoner again.

The taste of his own blood was familiar. The prison guards had been forever accidentally on purpose elbowing him in the face. Unlike them, this man hadn't masked his second blow as an accident. He'd punched Dyme in the mouth, loosening one of his newly veneered front teeth in the process, then he walked out and slammed shut the shed door.

Dyme barely remembered being dragged by his legs and dumped on a concrete floor. The snap of the lock brought him back to full consciousness. As he lay there listening for voices and sniffing the air, his eyes adjusted, and he could see a weak light from Connie's outdoor lights coming through the slats of the wood. Looking at the ceiling, he figured this room was about the same size as the cell where he had spent eighteen years in an Arkansas SuperMax prison called Varner.

This year and a half of freedom was in some ways harder than the years of incarceration. He had known what to expect in Varner. Out here in the free world everything was different, scary. In prison his only focus was his case, writing letters to Dawn, and getting out. Once free, he learned about a different kind of prison, the prison of expectation and of implied debt.

Dyme realized he was hog-tied in the wooden shed behind Connie Horton's house. He thought about her now, this woman activist, his wife's best friend, the person he and Dawn shared a house with, with whom she had founded Arkansans for Justice, AFJ, their charitable organization that raised money for the crusade to get him free. Connie was the reason he was in this shed and the reason he'd fought with Dawn. His forehead throbbed where the hunter had smashed him with the gun, and he could feel blood dripping from the wound. He couldn't do anything except wait, just like in prison, he was shackled, helpless, and waiting. That was familiar.

CONVICTED CHILD KILLER TAKES SANCTUARY IN WEST LITTLE ROCK

Over a month ago Sabbath Dyme fell off the celebrity radar. Not one word about him attending a book signing, no talks about his eighteen years in prison, no television interviews, no sightings with movie stars. He simply disappeared.

Lenne has learned he is living right under your noses in West Little Rock and you don't even know it. Why hasn't the LRPD notified the neighbors that Sabbath Dyme's in the area?

Celebrity ex-convict Dyme has taken sanctuary in a protected oasis. He lives in a house surrounded by woods that sits on the bank of Delphi Pond. He is less than two hundred yards, as the crow flies, from an upscale athletic club which has gymnastic and swim teams for children. There is a church daycare nearby, and a Starbucks, and a school bus stop. Considering the crime he was convicted of, Lenne thinks you deserve a heads-up.

And in case you somehow missed it: Sabbath Dyme and his accomplice were convicted in 1995 of killing three little boys in a wooded area called Pleasant Valley in the small town of West Memphis, Arkansas. The dead boys were hog-tied with their own shoelaces and left naked in the water for the turtles to munch on their soft parts.

**Maybe the LRPD does not know he is here.
That's a scary thought!**

Chapter 2

Delphi Pond - Dancing Bear - May 18, 2013 - 9:15 p.m.

Dyme rocked his body back and forth until he got as close to the door as he could. It was a hard journey with his hands tied to his feet. He wanted to get as far away from the back of the shed as possible, far away from the snakes that he imagined were nesting there. He would have preferred to be flat on his back, his favorite thinking position, but that was impossible. His body throbbed from his head to his feet.

Dyme sorted through the events of the day, trying to understand what had happened in his life that brought him here. But he knew the present would not bring him the answer he needed. The answer was in the past. The past made the present. His mind went back to that day on the deck when Connie had begun her systematic seduction of him by gaining his trust and making him physically comfortable with her alone in the hot tub. Water, the element present when every twisted event in his life happened.

The seduction took place over weeks but it had started about a month after he and Dawn arrived. Dawn had gone to visit her former landlady, Missy. Dyme had stayed home and soaked in the hot water, headset on, listening to Black River; even though they were not one of his favorite groups their lead singer, Seamus Doyle, was one of his favorite people. His money helped get Dyme out of prison and was still supporting his lifestyle. He opened his eyes to see Connie as she slipped her naked body in the tub and sat facing him. She brought her long arms up over her head, laced her fingers together, and stretched upward.

"I need a good soak," Connie said then shut her eyes and rested her head on the back of the tub.

He wasn't comfortable being naked in the tub alone with Connie, but he didn't want to jump right out and show it. Most things about women made him uncomfortable. He found them unpredictable and found himself unpredictable around them.

Connie opened her eyes. "I figured you needed a babysitter." She slid her foot under his leg. "Give me your foot. I'll do a little reflexology on you." She felt him resist. "Don't worry. It doesn't hurt." She took his foot and started kneading it, massaging, applying pressure to the acupuncture points.

As Connie worked on his feet, he relaxed. He thought of her flirting with him on her prison visits and worried she might start that again. She did not. The encounter was neutral, like a session he would have with a massage therapist, and he'd had plenty of those since getting out of prison, Dawn felt it would help his body heal. After five minutes or so, Connie got out of the tub and he didn't see her for the rest of the night.

It was only later he realized that was just the prelude of what was to come. Foreplay, it came in the form of innocuous hot tub soaks with Connie massaging his feet and listening to him like a therapist would as he spoke about his worries and his dreams. He looked forward to these therapy sessions, as he'd begun to think of them.

Connie knew his deep appreciation for her help setting him free. She'd given him a refuge here at the pond and one for Dawn too. Refuge, a safe harbor, a place where he had begun to relax for the first time since he'd gotten out. Then it came. Sex came after she'd made him feel safe.

The memory of his first sexual encounter with her still made him cringe. Dawn had been at her evening yoga workout at the athletic club when it happened. It was a night Connie usually came home late. He'd planned to spend the time alone working on a novel he was writing, but then Connie came home as soon as Dawn left.

She'd walked into the house with takeout from her restaurant, Trey's. "Surprise. I've brought all your favorites. I had to get out of there for a while and relax. I thought you might be hungry."

Connie sat on the sofa next to him and reached for the ceramic box that held her pot. She tapped a bud in the glass pipe, lit it, took a long hit, and passed it to him. It wasn't how he planned the evening. He needed privacy and quiet to write, but he went with it, went with what the evening presented to him, went with the flow. He'd smoked with her before although not many times and only with Dawn around. That should have been the first hint that this evening was going to be unlike all of their other times alone.

When the overture came, Dyme felt like he owed it to her, felt the weight of his debt, and he tried to give her what she'd wanted, but his erection was weak, it wouldn't hold. Connie didn't back off.

Connie said, "The French fuck with their face." And then she grabbed his head and firmly pushed him down. So that was how he had sex with Connie Horton the first time, with his face. Later came the Viagra and the rest of it.

Tonight, bound up like an animal in Connie's storage shed, the weight of all the expectations from everyone held him tighter than all the plastic ties. He owed everyone. He remembered Anna Blue, the Little Snoop, the morning she quoted the blogger Lenne Vee who had called him everyone's Dancing Bear.

Dancing Bear. He'd danced for Connie, for Dawn, for all of them. He let the memory of how he felt after that first sex with Connie wash over him again. He'd felt raped. That was the only way to put it, those feelings of not being in control but under her control. He'd felt guilty, the way a victim feels. He was a victim, he told himself, had always been a victim. A victim of his upbringing, of being different in a hick town, a victim of the sheriff, of the legal system, and now he could add that he was Connie Horton's victim.

Tied up like an animal on the damp concrete floor in the shed, he wished he had stayed in prison and waited for the new evidence, had another trial, and let a jury set him free. He would always be marked as the devil worshipping child killer who was convicted and then pled guilty to get out.

The pain in his body seemed to make his mind more clear as he laid there smelling the dirt and the mold in the shed, hearing who knows what crawling around. He thought about the way the fight with Dawn had started. There was something that didn't fit but he couldn't puzzle it out because his head began throbbing louder the more he tried to think and thoughts wouldn't stay in his mind long enough for him to thoroughly examine them.

Dyme closed his eyes and tried to get back in that moment. He saw Dawn standing on the deck bench. She seemed to wobble but then she had corrected her posture. He'd seen her do that little check in her balance before. The first time he had seen her walk along the top of the deck rail, it freaked him out. But she had acted like the rail was some kind of gymnastic bar and showed great balance. She had never fallen off that four inch wide rail to the pond twenty-four feet below. That was years of yoga training in action.

So there was the wobble. He had reached toward her. She was too far away for him to grab her hand. Then her body corrected itself and she steadied. Her eyes had connected with his, and then she went backward into the pond so easily that he didn't hear a splash. He didn't know if that was reality or a lucid dream.

Chapter 3

Delphi Pond - A Convict's Wife
- Spring - 2010

Three years earlier, on the day Sabbath Dyme's wife, Dawn Daniels, moved in with Connie Horton, Anna Blue learned from her neighbor Ron Cole that Dawn was married to a convicted child killer. Besides Anna and her parents, Maria and Richard Blue, Ron and his wife, Lisa, along with Dr. Billy and his wife and children lived on Delphi Pond. Anna had never heard of Sabbath Dyme, or his friend who was also convicted of the murders. Collectively the two convicts were known as the Pleasant Valley Two, the P.V. Two. Lisa Cole brought over a DVD of an HBO documentary about them. Anna watched it with her mother and Lisa.

Ron said, "I'm not watching anything about those trailer-trash baby killers. Those people are all inbred—it's no wonder. You watch, I am going on record right now, if he gets out, he will be living down here with Dawn and Connie. First it's the snakes, then the beavers. Hell, remember that alligator? Now it's the wife of a baby killer. Goddamn."

The producers of the HBO documentary thought the convicts, Sabbath Dyme and Jamie Ball, teenagers at the time, were victims of hillbilly lawyering and of ignorant, fearful jurors. The film was persuasive enough to attract the attention of some famous singers and actors, and over the years the P.V. Two had gotten plenty of attention from followers through their website. Still, they were not close to getting a new trial. Sabbath Dyme was now on death row and his clock was ticking down the fastest.

Dawn Daniels was a private person who'd only done one interview since she married Dyme. After watching the documentary, Anna searched the internet about the crime and read the interview that Dawn Daniels had given to Nora Ritt, who also wrote a book about the P.V. Two. Anna was thrilled about someone famous living on the pond and wanted to meet Dawn Daniels. Her mother told her to control her nosey nature and let their new neighbor get comfortable with the neighborhood.

So for a while, Anna did leave Dawn alone. She watched her from a distance. Spied on her. Anna found that when she tried to write a physical description of Dawn in her notebook, it was hard. Dawn was average in every way as far as Anna could tell. But then she'd only seen Dawn up close through her binoculars. Dawn's hair was neither dark blond nor light brown, it was somewhere in between. She'd put highlights in her hair some time ago, and they were fading.

Dawn wore her bangs cut to right above her eyebrows and the rest of her hair hung straight to the top of her shoulders. It clung to her head like a veil. Her height was medium and her body looked soft, but she could tell Dawn was strong since she moved big rocks while she worked on the shade garden she was building for Connie. Anna thought Dawn would make a good spy because she was so ordinary looking that she could not be accurately described.

Dawn had rituals. Every morning she soaked in the hot tub on the deck for fifteen minutes. She totally submerged herself under the water for two minutes, sometimes more. After the tub, she sat on a yoga mat in the lotus position and meditated for thirty minutes. She wrote in what Anna guessed was a journal every morning and evening and she spent a lot of time on her cell and the computer. While on the phone, she often played Scrabble with herself. She had the Onyx edition. After a month of watching, Anna walked around the pond to Connie's house.

"I just came to warn you. Ron Cole will probably take out his forty-five and shoot you for feeding the damn ducks." Anna did her best imitation of Ron Cole. "You are interfering with nature, you know, by feeding the damn squirrels and the damn raccoons."

The woman did not react in any way. She stood still and looked at Anna without an expression of any sort on her face. Anna could see assessment going on in her eyes and felt the coolness directed toward her.

Anna stammered. "I was just kidding about Mr. Cole. He wouldn't do that. It's just that he's always getting on me about feeding the wildlife. I'm Anna. I live across the pond."

Daniels shyly smiled, dipped her chin a little, and spoke in a quiet voice. "I just didn't know what to think; I haven't met any of the neighbors. I'm Dawn, a friend of Connie's."

When she smiled, Anna saw Dawn's only distinguishing feature. Her teeth were small for an adult and although they were evenly spaced, each one was a little far apart, especially the front ones.

Anna hung around and talked for a while. As the weeks passed, she would occasionally drop by when she saw Dawn outside and help her in the yard. They got into the habit of playing Scrabble once a week. No one mentioned Sabbath Dyme or the P.V. Two or anything close to it, but Anna went ahead and asked for a favor anyway.

"Our school is putting out its annual special edition paper. The articles are judged and only the winners are published. Will you let me interview you?"

"You want to write an article about me?" Dawn was more than a little surprised.

"Not about you, exactly. I am doing a piece on women who marry down. Professional women who marry, say, men in the trades. Wealthy women who marry poor men. Things like that. You're an educated professional woman who married an uneducated, younger man on death row. The article will feature three women. You will be one of them."

After what seemed like a long hesitation, Dawn spoke. "I'll think about it a few days and let you know. If I'm still on the fence, we'll play Scrabble and if you win, you get the interview." That worked for Anna. She wanted to compare the answers Dawn gave to her to the ones she had given to Nora Ritt. The interview would let Anna observe her without the distraction of yard work.

Dawn stayed on the fence but kept her word and Anna won their Scrabble game by nine points. After the interview, Anna listened to the tapes several times. She noticed that most of the answers Dawn gave sounded scripted and when she compared them to the Ritt article, they were almost verbatim.

"Why did you want to see the HBO documentary? I read that's how you got interested in the case, from the film."

"A good friend invited me to a film festival and the story of Sabbath and his friend was one of the documentaries we saw. I didn't know about the case before that. Afterward, we sat around talking about whether we thought the boys were innocent or guilty. We had different opinions.

"My friend didn't feel sorry for him. She said Sabbath came across as a self-consumed, preening, obnoxious know-it-all. He practically dared the sheriff to arrest him and the jury to convict him because at the trial he scoffed at the town and sneered at the jury. He even blew kisses from the witness box to the mothers of the dead boys. She said he was a typical eternal victim because he blamed the town of West Memphis for his conviction. She said she might have thought a little better of him if he'd acknowledged that his behavior helped convict him. Instead he claimed the town itself had convicted him before the jury did, just because he was different. They didn't understand him and didn't like that he dressed all in black. They didn't like his music and that he was a practicing Satanist. It was rumored that he killed small animals and drank their blood. I thought he was fairly creepy, at first, until I got to know him."

"What was your first impression of him from the film?"

"I agreed with MB, the friend I went with to the festival. I felt sorry for Jamie Ball. Sabbath had dropped out of school, but Ball was still in high school, trying to get out of the trailer park; he did have a bit of the troublemaker about him, but nothing serious. MB said that when Ball, who was Sabbath's best friend, was asked by a reporter if Dyme was innocent and he refused to say, that his non-answer was an answer. She had no sympathy for either of them."

"So, your friend, MB, did it hurt your friendship? Your two different views, I mean." Anna was curious about MB. In the time she'd known Dawn, she had never mentioned the name of any friend but Connie.

"No. Not at all. MB and I are opposites in so many ways. I sometimes think that's what makes us good friends. She's from New Orleans, a French Creole, and has that special way about her that comes from growing up there. Her name is really Morel Baptiste Bienville. That's a beautiful name, isn't it?"

"Sounds like a movie star," Anna agreed as she made a mental note to Google MB. "Since you thought Sabbath Dyme was arrogant, why did you write to him?"

Dawn gave what Anna recognized as scripted answer number one. "I felt a connection to him only after watching the film a number of times. Watching over and over saddened me. I found I couldn't stop thinking about it. I was so struck by the feeling that something was terribly wrong and after a while I absolutely believed in his innocence. I wrote him because he was in the most danger, on death row, and needed, desperately needed, an advocate. We wrote regularly for nearly a year before I came to Arkansas and met him. I wanted to get a feel for him other than as a pen pal."

"A year is a long time," said Anna.

"People think of women who write famous convicts as a type of celebrity stalker. They say we stalk prisoners because rock stars or movie stars would reject us. Prisoners can't get away and are grateful for our attention. We are seen as desperate women who desperately need to be needed. I didn't want to be seen that way. Then through reflection and meditation, I came to realize I was being selfish by staying away because I was afraid of what people would think of me."

"What was Varner SuperMax like?"

Dawn gave what Anna thought was scripted answer number two. "That awful prison was right in the middle of a huge dirt field. Maybe it had been a soybean or cotton field, I don't know. It was a series of structures low to the ground surrounded by electric wire fences, towers, and acres of open space. When I arrived guards admitted me to an exterior waiting room. The sounds and smells, the clanking of one door shutting before another opened, keys fitting into locks, the echoes, body odor, rancid air, all of it brought on a small fit of claustrophobia in me."

Dawn recalled a woman who looked exactly like she had imagined all the women who visited convicts looked like. "She touched my arm and I felt my nostrils flare and my skin crawl. Her Goodwill clothes were baggy on her skinny body, and her dirty hair, rotten teeth, and bad grammar reminded me of Sabbath's family and friends that I'd seen on the film, poor, uneducated people.

"I was dressed all wrong. I had wanted to appear sophisticated and unlike the other women who visited prisoners, but I overdressed. I wore a suit and a strand of pearls. What was I thinking? I remember so well this dirty woman, what she said. I won't forget it."

Dawn mimicked the country accent and grammar: " 'Ain't seen you here before. Who you here to see?' I said, 'I'm a friend of Sabbath Dyme's.' Then she said, 'Letter writin' friend who come to meet him for the first time, I suppose.' I said, 'How would you know that?' She said, 'I been comin' here a long time. Seen it all, I suppose. Most of the letter writin' girls come in here showin' a little skin, some shape, the men like that.' I said, 'Excuse me?' Then she insulted me. 'Most of 'em are a lot younger and prettier than you.'"

Anna had been impressed by the older woman's mimicry. She thought if she had shut her eyes, she wouldn't have known it was Dawn speaking.

Dawn said, "I had to remind myself this woman was suffering, she was ignorant, and that wasn't her fault. What could I expect dressed like I was? I began to wonder if I'd made a mistake. Then, as the universe would have it, the guard called my name and my destiny arrived.

"A guard took me to another room surrounded by thick glass. I thought he'd brought the wrong man, Sabbath looked so different from the film and the one picture he'd sent. He'd had his long hair cut short and lost his body fat. His cheeks were hollow now, not pudgy like when he first went in. All that was left of that Sabbath Dyme were his big dark eyes and slightly feminine gestures. When he saw me, his lips worked against each other in a slight pursing and relaxing motion. Like he was chewing his thoughts before he spoke them. I noticed that in the film too. He looked ill in his white prison pants and shirt. I wondered if he had cancer or AIDS.

"I waited for Sabbath to speak first. He kept chewing the inside of his lips, did the little pursing thing for a while, and finally he said, 'I feel like I'm on a blind date.' I replied, 'I feel like I've known you forever.' "

Anna had read in the Ritt article that by the time Dawn and Dyme met, they'd exchanged around two hundred letters. She wondered if that could be true. But then, all he had to do with his time was write letters. From what Dawn said in the interview, she loved writing to him. After meeting him in person, Dawn told her, like she'd told Ritt, she began sending Dyme hundreds of books on a wide range of subjects, Eastern philosophy, classics, biographies, the kinds of books an educated man would read. She sent so many books and CDs that if someone asked what Sabbath Dyme was up to in prison, they would hear that he was immersed in his reading and listening to Beethoven.

"Why did you leave a job as a professional landscape architect and marry a prisoner?" Anna figured this question would get scripted answer three.

"It wasn't my idea to get married. It was Sabbath's. After a while I saw the wisdom in it. He is wise. As a spouse I could do so much more for him than as a girlfriend or a supporter. Legally and financially. I could meet with the lawyers, set up fund-raising events, and manage the donations. I could act as his voice to the outside world. Since my marriage, I find that people listen to what I am saying. They look at me and think, 'She gave up a wonderful career in New York City and left her friends and family. She wouldn't have done that if he were guilty.' I have helped people change their minds about Sabbath. People need a reason to change. I feel fulfilled that he came into my life."

"Fulfilled?" Anna questioned. "So you don't feel like you married down?"

"My family did, especially my father, but they've come around. The idea of marrying down is so judgmental, don't you think? A friend of mine is an attorney and her husband works for the state. She makes hundreds of dollars an hour and his yearly salary is fifty thousand. But she doesn't feel like she's married down. They have a lot in common, like the things they read, their hobbies; they never run out of things to talk about. I feel the same about Sabbath."

"You mentioned you had a plan to help Sabbath and then said it was more of a calling. What do you mean?"

Dawn gave another scripted answer. "I meant a vision for fighting injustice. It is my calling. I am fighting for both of the men, not just Sabbath. Most importantly, I am bringing justice to the three little boys. Their murderers are still out there. I fight for every man or woman who has been victimized by the Arkansas justice system. Like a man is called to the priesthood, I've been called. This is my vocation. So yes, socially and financially I married down but in every other way Sabbath and I are equals."

Anna decided to push the point. "I guess someone could argue that he married down because he was a celebrity and well, you were not.

You were more a member of the support team or a groupie that married the star. Now that you are married, you are a celebrity of sorts yourself."

"I don't think I've thought of it that way before. Interesting point of view though. I let Connie be the star of the media show. You've known Connie all your life. I bet you can answer this. As a teenager, what did Connie want more than anything in the world? Well, now that I think about it, maybe she still does." Dawn gave a little laugh.

Anna felt this was Dawn's way of ending the interview. She had one more question and hoped she would have a chance to ask it.

"That is too easy. She wanted to be the first big movie star from Arkansas. My mom says that Connie has never gotten over that Mary Steenburgen, from North Little Rock, aka Dog Town back then, went to Hollywood and became a star. She says that's why Connie is always looking for ways to get herself in the paper. You know, she's been in the local paper in the society section almost a hundred times—she keeps a scrapbook. Just one more question though. When Sabbath gets out of prison, do you think you will stay married? I read that women who marry convicts are usually left behind when they get out. Do you worry about that?"

Dawn gave a serene smile, the kind Anna had seen on faces of people when they talked about Jesus and how he saved them. "No. I do not worry at all about being left behind. I trust the universe to take care of me."

Chapter 4

Stalking Connie Horton

Connie had lived on the bank of Delphi Pond for twenty-five years; the house and one acre lot had been a gift from her parents. She thought of Delphi as her sanctuary and the pond as her giant reflection pool. Yet she had invited a stranger into her oasis without knowing a thing about the woman who would share it with her.

When Dawn first moved to Little Rock, she had lived in the Quapaw Quarter in an old mansion turned into a triplex and owned by Missy McShane, whose family had lived in Little Rock for many generations. Missy arranged for Dawn's job as a landscape architect at the Arkansas Parks and Recreation Department. She didn't know Dawn didn't have a degree or certification in that field. Dawn had only practical experience working for a landscape nursery and a talented amateur eye for design. No one asked to see any documentation. The recommendation from Missy and a social security number got her the job. Dawn worked there for two years and it was during this time that public interest in the crusade to free the P.V. Two began to slip and donations along with it.

When the public loses interest in a worthy cause it can become a hopeless one. This cause needed help and so Dawn called MB Bienville, who made her first trip to Little Rock. MB stayed at the Peabody in the downtown area instead of bunking with Dawn. MB was a poker aficionado and she had a better chance of picking up a game at the Peabody than at the Hampton Inn in West Little Rock or Missy McShane's. MB had been there nearly ten days before she gave Dawn her assessment and recommendation.

"Honey, you got too many celebrities and not enough community involvement. Most people from around here don't care a snit about Sabbath Dyme. Big names and out-of-state people who are interested in a cause don't move locals, especially in the South. You need to start a grassroots crusade and team up with someone who has a high profile around here. We need to take the online activism and spread it off-line. Go personal. Put a local face on things. Get a broader audience. See what I mean?"

Dawn pushed her salmon around the plate, searching for the little new potatoes sprinkled with fresh dill. "I see. The P.V. Two website is active, but it doesn't bring in enough donations and it can't influence people who aren't into internet searching and blogging. Therefore the website can't influence the legal system around here or the politicians or the people. Makes sense."

MB continued, "What I am saying is that you need a high profile, local best friend. Has to be a woman otherwise everyone will speculate about sex and that would be a distraction. Professional woman with contacts. No country club type with a banker husband, if you know what I mean. Rich women with nothing else to do will alienate the worker bees. A high profile professional, that's number one on the list. Number two. Shift the emphasis toward the broader topic of injustice and de-emphasize Dyme and the other guy. Fight for the dead little boys, justice for them, find their real killers, and of course a new trial. Injustice is something churches can get their teeth into and this looks like the land of the fundamentalist to me. The size of some of these churches, gluttonous. Get the preachers involved too."

Dawn let out a long sigh and stabbed a potato. "Got it. I need to make changes to get local support. Blend social media with the personal touch. It's not like the old days with Mama and her causes. That was all personal touch. Today it is both. You've got a good point. We've been top heavy with the online activism. I see that now. I'll try it, but I'm giving it a deadline too. I married Sabbath six years ago, moved here around two years later, and I've had enough of prison and lawyers and bloggers and the press. That's the bad thing about social media. Everything is so in your face and immediate. I figure I've got about two more years of this left in me."

MB handed her a file on a Connie Leigh Horton. "Born in Little Rock, in her fifties, owns a restaurant called Trey's in the right end of town that's been around about twenty years. She's a fifty-fifty partner with her ex, Beau Bowen, who is also a well-connected local. Best of all, she is a publicity whore and that makes my work a whole lot easier."

Dawn nodded. "I read a profile of her in the local paper. It was a special they were doing for restaurant month, featuring a different venue every week. The article had a half page picture of Connie Horton lying on her back in a mess of produce. Carmen Miranda with veggies. Missy knows her, knew her grandmother. She showed me the article. Missy has lunch with her old biddies at Trey's once a week. I've never been in there."

"I hired a local investigator to fill in what I had on Horton. She talked to people from Horton's grade school, high school, and her former employees. Checked out where she gets pedicures, massages, her fitness club, favorite restaurants, where she grocery shops, so on.

"What I suggest is you start going for supper at Trey's on the nights she works late. Court her. She responds to women and men in that way. She will be attracted to you because you are a minor celebrity and your cause is edgy, movie stars and singers are involved. She wants to be a big name herself and her only means is her restaurant."

"You are amazing," Dawn said.

"It wasn't me. The investigator was great and Connie Horton has hurt many feelings around this town."

Dawn paged through the file. "This is interesting. Connie's suing her father's widow over a piece of artwork. She started the suit less than six months after he died of a sudden heart attack. That was only eight months ago. Sounds like she might need a best friend and a worthy cause to ease the pain."

MB added, "An Alexander Calder. Three million. I called Connie's stepmother and told her I worked for the *Arkansas Times,* asked her for a comment. You know what she said? 'My name isn't Connie. She's the attention seeker. Call her. You will probably get paragraphs.' "

"Um. I don't like Connie. You can't trust her," said Dawn.

"Why exactly?"

Dawn took a minute and flipped back through the file. "She cheated on both her husbands with the hired help and let them catch her in the act. That's a little mean. Looks like several of her old friends reported this to your investigator and to me that means she's probably done something to them or they wouldn't be telling it. That says trust issues."

"That's what I said. She has hurt a lot of feelings around this town. We don't have to trust her, just use her, and that'll be easy. Her ego is gigantic. Now I have to tell you about what I've been up to.

"Last night I met a few brokers from Stephens and Crews here in the bar. I've been seeing them around this week. When I heard them talking, I knew it was about poker. I eased myself into the conversation and before long, they invited me to their game upstairs. I am fifteen thousand richer this morning. They want a chance to win it back tonight and I am happy to oblige."

"Glad to see you're keeping your skills sharp. So I guess I won't see you this evening."

"I have to keep sharp and sharper. Don't forget I'm going to Vegas in about ten days for the big tournament. Besides, you need to start studying. There is a lot here about Horton and the family antique collection. That's just one of the ways into her heart."

That evening and for several after, Dawn studied the Horton file. She started the courtship the way MB suggested and began eating at Trey's every week or so. It didn't take long before Dawn and Connie became friends. Connie got interested in the cause, and Dawn increased her interest by having Sabbath send her a letter asking her to visit him in prison so he could thank her personally. Connie made several visits to Varner and enjoyed telling her friends about them as a way of recruiting them to the cause.

Dawn and Connie worked as an efficient team and after two years of their lobbying, the state of Arkansas released the P.V. Two from prison. Dawn and Sabbath left from Memphis the next day on a private jet provided by his celebrity supporters. After half a lifetime in an Arkansas prison, Sabbath wanted to get out of the state and out of the South as quickly as he could. His release was polarizing to Arkansans and he feared vigilantes.

The sudden departure of Dyme and Dawn gave Connie her chance to shine all on her own. Connie loved being on television without Dawn, seeing herself quoted in the blogs and the papers and on the news. She had never liked sharing. In her latest interview, which took place at Trey's on the patio, a reporter asked, "Are you going for a pardon?"

Connie didn't hesitate. "Definitely!" She didn't have a clue about what a pardon involved or if the men were eligible. But it sounded like a good idea and she didn't want to appear out of the loop.

The deal that the P.V. Two made with the state was called an Alford plea. The men pled guilty while they maintained their innocence and got out for time served with a ten year suspended sentence. In exchange they could not sue the state of Arkansas. That was about all Connie knew and even that had to be explained to her a couple of times before it sank in. It seemed so contradictory.

Now that Sabbath and Dawn were out of the state, Connie found herself at the helm. She could make the decisions. She had Beau put the idea of a pardon out on the P.V. Two website for the supporters and bloggers to chew over. The response was unanimous among supporters. They wanted the pardon but of course Dyme haters scoffed at the idea.

Connie wondered why Dawn wasn't working on it already. Maybe she was. Connie didn't know what went on in Dawn's mind. She was private to the point of paranoia and Connie had once said this to her.

Dawn had responded in an even tone, like a teacher explaining to a child. "Connie, you put your whole life on the internet. There is so much about you out there that a third rate con could steal your identity. Look around your own home. This prize collection of yours. It's probably worth millions and the whole world knows about it. Everyone knows your mother's maiden name, your grandmother's, where you went to school, and on and on. I worry about someone taking advantage of you."

Dawn wanted to say, *All that information you so willingly put out to the public brought me to your door, and you don't even know who you invited into your home.*

Connie resented the remark about a third rate con. Dawn made her sound like a fool. So she Googled Dawn Daniels, something she'd never done, and could not find one personal thing beyond what Connie already knew. It was like she didn't have a past or a life before Sabbath and the P.V. Two. Connie didn't think much past that. Dawn had been a find for her. Since meeting Dawn, her life had become exciting. Hanging out with celebrities and martyred convicts filled a need in her. She was getting past the age of seducing the kitchen help and this was a new kind of fun.

Connie wanted AFJ, Arkansans for Justice, to turn its mighty donation machine toward a pardon now that freedom had been obtained. A
pardon would keep the cause alive and Connie needed that. She didn't
want to be left behind now that Dyme was free. Her life would go
back to working at Trey's, catering weddings, a vacation twice a year,
and riding her bicycle over the Big Dam Bridge on the weekends. She
couldn't hang out with celebrities or go to New York for fund-raisers.
Life would become empty again. A pardon was good for everyone, especially Connie.

Dawn and Dyme were in Seattle when the call Connie told them to
expect came through.

When Dawn picked up, Connie said in an excited voice, "Turn on
CNN."

They did and saw Connie sitting on the red sofa in her living room,
in a pair of shorts, on the telephone, with a reporter in the room. Connie
said, "We miss you down here. We love you. Boy, have I got big news.
We are going for a full pardon. Full pardon, baby. Full pardon! We're on
a wave and we've going to take this ride to shore." She whooped and
the camera moved in closer.

Connie hit a button and announced, "We're on speaker."

The reporter said, "Is Sabbath with you? Do you have a comment?"

Connie had gone rogue. Once committed, Connie had thrown herself into the fight full force and it looked like she was becoming her
own reality show. Dawn hadn't figured on the depth of Connie's need
to be needed or her greater need to be noticed, to perform. Horton had
a web of friends and customers throughout Little Rock. She reached out
to all of them and in turn they reached out to their friends. She worked
it like a giant pyramid scheme. Connie was a natural.

"Hello, this is Dawn." She spoke in a very low voice, loud enough to
be barely heard but not understood.

Connie said, "We can't hear you. Speak up. I can't hear. Wait. I'll
take it off speaker, maybe that will help."

"Connie, what the hell are you doing? You can't make that decision
without me. There are repercussions. Get off that subject right now. We
will talk later about it."

Dawn watched the television. Connie was smiling and nodding her
head.

"Okay. Okay. Great. Now remember, when Sabbath gets tense rub his shoulders. Do what I showed you. Press those acupressure points. I love you guys." Connie made little kissing sounds in the phone and hung up while she smiled at the camera.

The reporter said, "This governor is not going to just hand over a pardon. Pardon will be an expensive fight."

Connie looked into the camera and sat up straight. "We've got the money, baby, and we got the fight in us." She gave a little fist pump.

Dawn gave out a groan. "That woman doesn't know how to keep her mouth shut."

Dyme didn't agree. He thought Connie had made a great move and said so.

Dawn replied, "You cannot tell people you've got the money to fight and expect them to continue to contribute. This thing costs money, Sabbath. We need the donations. Connie doesn't understand how it works."

"I think she's doing a good job. I like the image about riding the wave to shore and the fist pump. That's positive."

"Leave the contributions and how to get them to me. Bragging is not a good thing in this business. Humility is. Connie is off base. Believe me on that."

The next phone call came from MB. "Get that dumb Horton bitch under control. She's just bragged the coffers are full enough to go after a pardon. Kelly Dudley is asking questions and there are more rumblings about AFJ's lack of financial transparency on the blogs and in the newspapers. This is not good."

"I think we spawned a monster. Sabbath and I are talking it over," letting MB know she couldn't speak freely.

After the call ended Sabbath asked who'd called and Dawn said, "Our event planner." Dyme didn't know the history of MB and Dawn. He knew very little about his wife.

"What did you mean 'spawned a monster'?"

"I meant it in a good way, sweetie. Like Connie really goes for it. She makes a monster effort. That sort of thing," Dawn explained, pissed at herself for making the crack in front of him.

The interview did spawn a call from Lynn Hertz with *Little Rock Business* magazine. AFJ had never been interviewed by the publication and Connie figured that rag was just getting on board with the hippest cause Little Rock had ever seen. Hertz came to the pond to interview Connie and she was pleased as it gave her a chance to show off her collection of art and antiques.

Hertz was supposed to ask about the upcoming event to raise money for the P.V. Two pardon but somehow the interview slid off into AFJ's finances. As director, Connie signed the 990's and checks. The details about finances were Dawn's department. It hadn't occurred to Connie that as the director she would be held accountable if they were audited.

Hertz asked, "You've said publicly that the AFJ already has the money to fight for a pardon. Correct?" Connie nodded yes. "Then why the aggressive drive for donations now?"

"We feel we have the funds needed but there are so many unexpected costs in the drive for exoneration that we don't want to come up short. It is better to be prepared. When the fight is over, AFJ will donate what is left to other unjustly imprisoned men and women." That just came to Connie and she thought it brilliant.

Lynn Hertz was a former financial reporter from LA who had moved to Little Rock ten years earlier and gone to work for *Little Rock Business* magazine more as a hobby than a job while she raised her sons. She had a knack for finding the story and she knew the newspaper business. When her sons entered grade school, she went to work full-time and was now the publisher. Her husband was a special agent with the Internal Revenue Service. Connie didn't know this and neither did many other people. If Connie had Googled her, which Hertz figured she would since that was what most people did, she would find nothing linking Hertz to the IRS.

"Over the past year, there have been three requests from Kelly Dudley, and two other former contributors to the AFJ, for a public accounting from your organization but you have refused. Why is that?"

"I... I don't know what you are referring to." Connie felt a little stammer in her speech.

"To refresh your memory." Hertz handed Connie copies of several articles.

Connie glanced at the first headline: "Supporters of P.V. Two Feud Over Funds for the Defendants." She glanced down at the highlighted sentences.

*P.V. Two freedom fund squabble grows.
*Supporters raise millions. Where does it go?
*AFJ still hasn't given a public accounting of the money.
*Nora Ritt aims criticism at Dawn Daniels and Connie Horton.
*Kelly Dudley, former contributor to AFJ, forms rival fund-raising group that claims total financial transparency and challenges AFJ to do the same.

One pink highlight hung in the air for Connie: **You have to wonder about a woman who quits her job in NYC to move to Arkansas and marry a guy on death row, don't you? What's in it for her other than the millions she's controlling?**

Connie was in over her head and smart enough to know it. She looked at her watch. She raised her eyebrows and opened her eyes wide then gave Lynn an apologetic look.

"I need to wrap it up. Got to get to Trey's." She tapped the face of her new watch.

"We agreed to an hour and it's only half gone. I just have a couple more questions."

The reporter handed Connie a copy of her mortgage and the release. Connie felt her hand tremble as she took them and hoped Hertz hadn't seen it. She was so nervous she vibrated. Connie took a few seconds to do one of her calming exercises, opened her nostrils and breathed slowly in, out, in, out.

"This is my personal business. What are you doing with it?" Connie was glad she had taken the calming breath even if it hadn't helped much. She stood up to her full five foot ten inches and tied and untied her ponytail, a certain indicator of her tension, then walked to the kitchen for water, ignoring the pitcher of ice water on the table in front of them.

"Public information. You had an existing mortgage on your home when you and Daniels founded AFJ. In 2011, you paid it off. Did that money come from AFJ's legal fund?"

"Of course not."

Connie could not tell Hertz that paying off the mortgage with AFJ funds had been Dawn's idea. She had said it would be legitimate compensation for two years of AFJ rent, using the house to conduct interviews and fund-raising events. It had been Beau's idea to mortgage the house to pay for the remodel. Now that mistake was coming back to haunt her, just like her daddy had told her it would when he found out about it. Connie was grateful Hertz did not know about the Calder mobile that she had purchased with AFJ funds. Technically it belonged to AFJ, even though the bill of sale was in her name. If push came to shove, she could list the piece as an AFJ asset on the next 990.

"The supporters who are asking for transparency also have these documents and, considering the economy and the fact most of the restaurants in town, including yours, are fifteen percent down, they will ask that question," said the reporter.

"Lynn, I don't know if you read the *Memphis Commercial Appeal*. Not long ago they did an article on this. Dawn declined to discuss the details of the funds but she said that there were no complaints from defense lawyers on how donations were handled. That should be good enough for you."

Hertz replied, "The lawyers wouldn't complain if they were getting paid. According to my research, the legal fees are being privately and directly paid by a few celebrities. Calls to their publicists confirmed it. So the question now is how much donation income from AFJ is being converted to personal use?"

Connie stared at Hertz. She'd misjudged this small dumpy woman. Dawn would have known what Hertz was about and ignored her. In fact, that's just what Dawn had been doing.

Hertz pushed on. "I hear whispers that the attorney general has a complaint on his desk regarding the AFJ so you might need to explain it to him. The IRS also might want to audit your personal books and Trey's as well."

Connie felt sick at the mention of the attorney general, the complaint, the possible audit. All she wanted at this moment was for this woman to leave.

As if on cue, Lynn Hertz stood, picked up her things, and turned toward the door. She looked around the room. She recognized it as the room that Connie Horton and Dawn Daniels used for their interviews. It was a set, aimed to impress. She touched the red lacquered Korean chest with the bust of a Ming dynasty official sitting on top.

Hertz said, "Georges Braque's *Nature Morte aux Citrons*," indicating the painting over the chest. Her pronunciation was perfect.

Connie puffed up a bit with pride. "It was my grandfather's."

There was an array of travel books on a cloverleaf side table, objects from all over the world were placed around the room, an antique desk, a wall of bookshelves with well-worn books and small objects. Designed to say a lot without the owner saying a thing.

Worn books say you are an avid reader; art says you are a collector; objects from various cultures say you are a sophisticated traveler. Hertz got the picture. She didn't comment on the massive tapestries, the custom cabinets housing a pre-Columbian pottery collection, and other art works. She'd read about Horton's collection. She would not mention it. Then the air conditioner came on, and the Calder mobile that hung near an air vent moved and caught Hertz's eye. She looked up. "Is that an Alexander Calder?"

Connie wanted to say lie and say no, it was a reproduction, but her ego wouldn't let her, so she said instead, "Yes. That is a Calder. My father left it to me."

"I thought I saw that you were suing your stepmother over your father's Calder. I believe she sold it and that was when you filed suit. We had a piece about it in our Whispers section. Are you saying that this is the same piece of work?"

"That was a different one." Connie wished that she had simply said no, it was not authentic. Dawn told her once that liars usually gave themselves away with too much information.

"Is this a recent purchase?" Hertz pursued.

"No."

"Your father owned more than one?" Before Connie could react, Hertz had snapped a picture of the piece with her cell phone.

"You can't come in here and photograph my things. I resent that."

Hertz slipped the cell back into her jacket pocket. "You allow television cameras in here during your interviews. I've seen your entire living room and its contents on the news many times. Surely you don't object to my admiring your Calder. Not many people get to see one of these mobiles except in galleries or museums."

"Please leave. I have to get to work." Connie walked toward the front door and opened it. She felt light-headed and a little winded.

Connie wanted to push Lynn Hertz down the steep steps and throw her body in the pond for the turtles to eat. Someone had put a baby alligator, or maybe it was a crocodile, in the pond once, and when it got big enough to notice, Ron Cole shot it. Connie fervently wished it was grown and still living there.

September 1, 2012

CON ARTISTS LOVE NONPROFIT ORGANIZATIONS

There are approximately 1.6 million nonprofit organizations registered in this country. This figure doesn't include the 700,000 churches and small charities that are not required to register.

Nonprofit organizations control over 4 TRILLION dollars in the United States.

Nonprofit exemptions and tax benefits to donors cost the U.S. Treasury 100 BILLION dollars a year.

Nonprofits place second in major embezzlements in this country. The financial sector is first.

Given these facts, I am not surprised that a growing number of Arkansans for Justice donors are asking why the organization will not give a public financial accounting. Kelly Dudley, who was once a contributor to AFJ, has aggressively pressed Daniels for transparency, as have many others. Daniels refuses to respond to any financial questions. What she does say, "My attorney is happy with how I handle the funds."

I have run across the 990 forms for AFJ on a public site. Take a look.

2011 Form 990 - *Return of Organization Exempt from Income Tax under Section 501(c) of the Internal Revenue Code.* It was signed by Connie Horton.

Line 17 - "Other expenses" .... $ 270,250

That number matches the release of the mortgage on the Horton home in 2011.

No wonder there are questions.

September 10, 2012

LETTER TO EDITOR - *ARKANSAS DEMOCRAT-GAZETTE*

Arkansans might appreciate a lesson on how nonprofit organizations work. The *Democrat-Gazette* should do this as a service to its subscribers.

A nonprofit organization is commonly used by cons to prey on a community's willingness to help. The public often assumes these organizations are heavily regulated and this is true if regulation means initial paperwork. Once a nonprofit has filed its application under the 501(c), the organization does not have to make public how much money is raised or how it is distributed or what percentage goes to the cause or to the board members.

Since it has been high profile in Arkansas lately, I will use Arkansans for Justice, AFJ, as an example of how a nonprofit works. Dawn Daniels, Connie Horton, and Beau Bowen formed AFJ for the benefit of the Pleasant Valley Two. They are the board members. The purpose of a board is to keep the organization ethical. Consider this: Daniels lived with Horton for two years. Bowen is Horton's ex-husband and business partner. This is the fox watching the henhouse.

People give willingly. Would they continue to donate to nonprofit organizations if they knew how the money was spent?

It is not enough to state the "funds are handled with integrity" such as Daniels did through her New York publicist when Dudley and others requested transparency.

I urge the *Arkansas Democrat-Gazette* to do the community a service and ask for a public accounting from every nonprofit in the state that collects over one million a year.

Chapter 5

Delphi Pond - Dawn and Sabbath - Winter - 2013

D r. Billy and his wife, Lou, were having a neighborhood dinner party in their "Florida Room" the evening Dawn brought Sabbath Dyme to the pond to live. It was the dead of winter, ice on the water. In the Florida Room, a large greenhouse made of insulated glass walls and skylights, it was eternal summer. Dr. Billy had dubbed it the Florida Room many years ago when he and his wife had decided to build it instead of buying a condo in Florida and the name had stuck.

As the neighbors sat around sipping drinks and eating appetizers, they watched as a black stretch limo drove slowly down the long drive to Connie Horton's house. It parked under the deck where Connie usually kept her car. A driver got out, then Dawn Daniels, and then four men. The driver brought up several bags from the car to the house. Connie pulled in beside the limo. She catapulted out of the car and jumped up and down with excitement, hugging and kissing Dawn and hugging a man Anna identified as Sabbath Dyme. First a crocodile and now a convict. What was the pond coming to?

Cole kept a little pair of binoculars in his hunting vest, a garment he was never without, and he already had the glasses out. He said, "Well, I'll be goddamned. Connie's brought that baby killer down here. Her daddy must be rolling in his grave. I predicted it, I warned y'all. Aren't perverts supposed to register or something? Lisa, have we got any notices about a child killer moving in the neighborhood?"

Dr. Billy said, "Ron, that's sex offenders that have to register and besides Jim was cremated and his ashes scattered by helicopter in the Gulf of Mexico. Just because there is luggage doesn't mean they are moving here."

"Bet you it does. Isn't killing three eight-year-old boys, hog-tying them with their own shoelaces, and leaving them in a drainage ditch enough of a crime to get a killer on a neighborhood watch list? Billy, you should be worrying about that pervert living down here. Hell, man, you got three little girls about the ages of those boys he killed." Ron handed the glasses to Anna who had her hand outstretched. He then poured himself another Woodford Reserve.

"You are not going to believe this, Mom. Seamus Doyle and that guy, what's his name from the *Hobbit*, are with them. Connie will definitely need her Depends."

"Anna."

"Mom. I saw the box. It was sticking out of the garbage can. When garbage is on the street it is public property. The police can go through it without a warrant. Anyway. I just peeked inside the can."

"Hon, give Ron back his glasses. And, you, quit encouraging her." Maria wagged her finger in Ron's direction.

The next morning Anna started her surveillance on Dyme. Like his spouse, Sabbath Dyme had rituals. In spite of the cold, every morning he paddled Connie's canoe to the middle of the pond and watched the sun rise. In the evening, he did the same to watch it set. He did at least a hundred push-ups twice a day on the deck in front of the master suite. One thing he did not do was make any effort to meet the neighbors.

Anna noticed the couple led parallel lives. She had her rituals and he had his; they didn't do much of anything together. Dawn did the same things as she had before, except she didn't have cocktail time with Connie in the hot tub any longer. Dyme had a cell phone and a laptop that Anna rarely saw him use.

After weeks of watching Anna watch Dyme paddle around the pond, Maria Blue made a decision.

Maria said to her husband, "Honey, I'm going to invite Dawn and Sabbath Dyme over for coffee. I need to have a sense of him if he is going to live around us."

Richard looked up from his routine breakfast of an egg white sand-wich with salsa on Ezekiel toast. He was a conservative man by nature, being an attorney, an accountant, and a former officer in the Marine Corps. At age forty, Richard still kept his medium height and frame body in excellent condition by running and a strict diet. He kept his hands and feet healthy with a regular manicure and pedicure.

"Leave him alone," said Richard. "If he's still around in the spring, you may run into him. That would be natural."

"Maybe it would be better to have a neighborhood brunch instead of a one on one."

"Please, Maria. Let it go. Don't indulge her. I just can see it now, you and Anna interrogating him." Richard kissed Maria, walked out in the cold morning to start up his Porsche 911-Carrera-4s, his only extravagance. Maria would not let it go, he knew that, and she didn't.

After Anna got home from school and had her usual snack of non GMO popcorn and organic lemonade, Maria sent her to Connie's house with a note inviting Dyme and Dawn over for coffee that coming Saturday. Richard would be doing a 10K run but Anna would be home. Between the two of them, they would get a feeling about Sabbath Dyme.

Anna slipped the note under the front door. As soon as it disappeared, the door opened and Dyme stood in front of her. Anna was startled into speechlessness, an uncommon condition for her. Her eyes traveled the length of his body and back up to his swept-back black hair. Dyme wore rose tinted glasses in sequenced frames like Deepak Chopra and loose black slacks, but his chest was bare, as were his feet.

Anna gasped a little. His death white skin was marked with doz-ens of dark tattoos which covered his upper body like armor. Her eyes traveled over the tribal bands, angels, demons, Phoenix rising, Celtic crosses, and knots. The designs started at his neck and ran the length of his arms and across his chest and stomach and she imagined they crossed his back and down his legs.

Anna took it in and he stood there and let her. She said, *"The Illustrated Man."*

Dyme said, "Who?"

Anna kept her eyes on his body as she spoke. *"The Illustrated Man.* Short tales written by Bradbury in 1951 and made into a movie in the early sixties. It's the story of a man covered in tattoos that were inked on his body by a woman time traveler. Each one told a tale. I am surprised it wasn't one of the hundreds of books Dawn sent you in prison. It's a modern classic in its genre."

"I thought Bradbury wrote children's books. How does a kid like you care about movies that came out before you were even born?"

"He did write some books for kids, that's right. And old movies are one of my hobbies. *The Illustrated Man* is something you would probably like. It's really dark and the tattoos come alive and tell tales of woe. I think you can still get it on NetFlicks."

Anna looked at the envelope in his hand. "My mom wanted me to give you that."

"You are Anna. Right?"

"How did you know that?"

"Dawn filled me in on the neighbors." Dyme opened the envelope and looked at the note, slowly reading the precise handwriting. "Tell your ma we will let her know. I'll have to talk to Dawn. She's the decider." His lips pursed and relaxed and moved a little side to side.

Anna recognized the tic from the documentary about him and the interviews she'd seen on the internet. "Thanks. I'll tell Mom."

Anna looked past Dyme into the living room. Her eyes lifted to the ceiling and took in the Calder mobile hanging from a monofilament line. The air from the heat vent made it move slightly and attracted her attention.

"Sabbath Dyme free as an autumn leaf floating on a breeze."

"What?"

Anna explained, "Connie put a photo on her Facebook page of you with that mobile. I was quoting the caption."

"Oh, yeah. I remember now. I was hanging it back up after we cleaned it. It's a little hard to manage because it wiggles around. Dawn helped me. Connie calls it her centerpiece."

"I guess you and Connie have that in common. Collecting, I mean. You collect tattoos on your body and she collects art."

"I hadn't thought about that before."

"I hope you and Dawn come over. See ya." Anna turned and walked away.

Maria was a short, trim woman who didn't wear makeup except for a little mascara because her skin was creamy and smooth. Her preferred outfit was a skort with a form fitted shirt and Dansko clogs for added height. She wore her blond hair cut very short and combed back away from her high forehead. Maria Blue looked smart and she was. Two PhDs, one in psychology and the other in sociology. She worked for herself as a jury consultant and considered herself an excellent reader of body language. She recognized when a man was weary and sick at heart and knew she was looking at one standing in her door, a study in black.

Sabbath Dyme wore tight black jeans tucked into black boots, a black laced-up poet shirt, and a black leather duster. He wore black framed rectangular glasses with yellow lenses. Maria extended her hand, not as a handshake but as a welcoming gesture.

"Come on in. We'll sit by the fire."

"Dawn couldn't come. She told me I should meet you, so here I am."

Told told Maria a lot. "Good to meet the neighbors. Never know when we might need each other, right?" She smiled to set him at ease.

Dyme didn't respond as he followed her into the den. He took the chair she gestured toward.

Anna looked him up and down as she walked into the room. "Wow. *Pirates of the Caribbean* meets *The Good, the Bad and the Ugly*. I like the duster. The leather is a twist. Do you know why your coat is called a duster?"

"No, but I bet you do."

"Originally these long coats were made of canvas or linen and worn by horsemen to protect their clothing from dust. Standard issue for Texas Rangers."

"Dawn said you were full of information." Dyme accepted the double espresso and the biscotti Maria offered and waited. He wished Dawn hadn't changed her mind at the last minute. This wasn't his scene. He was figuring he would give it thirty minutes at the most, when he realized Maria Blue was speaking to him.

"I would not have guessed you would come back to the state. Most people thought you would stay in LA or Seattle. Maybe New York or even New Zealand. What brought you back here?"

Dyme used the tips of his fingers to push his glasses up higher on his nose before he answered. "My publicist advised against it and my attorney did too. We've got tons of fund-raising work to do for the pardon. But I'm worn out. I haven't had an hour to myself since I got out except the time I've spent on the pond."

Maria told him, "You do look tired. I can't imagine being incarcerated for eighteen years and then with just two days' notice being set free. How are you coping?"

"Being busy helped. I got a driver's license, and an iPhone, and I've been all over the place. Before prison, I'd never been on an airplane or outside the state at all." He talked about what he had learned and had to learn and after he'd said it once, he went over it again. It was anxious talk.

"Me and Dawn went to so many parties and events and places. She would hand me a schedule every morning, where we were going, who to see. It got to be too much. In prison, I sat alone all day. I wore one set of clothes. Now, I have people who carry my bags and I have dozens of shirts and pants and shoes and glasses. My supporters want to touch my arm, shake my hand, put an arm around my shoulders."

In her mind, Maria filled in the rest of what he did not say... *And I don't like being touched.*

"So you needed a vacation from your exciting life?" Anna asked.

"I need time to figure out who I am instead of being told who I am. I am a free man but feel like I'm in a box. My life feels small and, well, I thought it would feel big."

"You are a dancing bear. That's why you feel that way."

"Anna!" Maria gave her daughter The Look which was the warning to watch her mouth, control her words.

"Mom. I'm just quoting from one of Lenne Vee's blogs. I can quote it, 'Dyme's everyone's moneymaker. Everyone who helped him has a piece of him. He owes them all. Sabbath Dyme is their dancing bear.' "

That took the air out of the room.

Dyme stood up, stretched his back, and walked to the sliding glass door. He looked out at the pond a long time. He stood with his hands clasped behind his back staring across at the Horton house. Back still turned, he said to no one in particular, "The pond is a little spooky. It's got ghosts. I sometimes hear them moan."

Maria broke his mood. She didn't really like small talk. It was always a challenge for her at parties. Anna's commentary sparked something in her and she asked Dyme a question.

"Sabbath, do you read *Little Rock Business* magazine?"

He turned toward her. "Ma'am, I stay away from the news in any form. Nothing good there."

Maria Blue picked up the paper from the end table and turned to the Lynn Hertz article. "Here." She handed him the paper.

Dyme didn't sit. He took it from her hand and walked back to the glass door where he stood and read it. Anna noticed his lips moved and he took his time. What would have taken her less than five minutes to absorb took him more than ten.

"I didn't know about this Hertz reporter. I know Dawn can't stand that Kelly guy who keeps asking the questions about AFJ finances. A while back she said he was trying to discredit her because he had a fund-raising organization that was a competitor for our donations."

"He's not the only one asking," Maria said.

"Like I said, I don't know. That's what Dawn does."

Anna noticed Dyme became more uncomfortable the longer he stayed, and she didn't want him to leave. She wanted to engage him in a conversation.

So Anna changed the subject. "Dawn let me interview her for a class project. My article was one of those picked for the special edition paper at school."

"She's extremely private about herself. You must be persuasive."

"No. I didn't persuade her. She lost a bet, a Scrabble game, and the interview was my prize. When I was typing it up, I wondered how you got the courage to ask her to marry you. How did you?"

"You mean because I was a white trash convicted murderer and she was a sophisticated landscape architect from New York City?"

"Yeah."

"Anna," warned Maria and gave her another look.

"No, it's okay," Dyme said to Maria. "It didn't take courage. She asked me. More like she told me. She got it into her mind early on that we should get married. Said it was the best way for her to help me."

"Oh. The interview she did with Nora Ritt didn't say who did the asking and that was why I wondered." Anna also wondered who was telling the truth.

She continued to question him. "I've read the Dyme Letters on the P.V. Two website. How did you come up with that idea? You sound like a therapist when you are writing to some of your supporters."

Dyme looked at this seventeen-year-old girl, so small yet older than her years, curious, bold. Her mother made him uncomfortable but

Anna made him feel like a fraud. He waited to answer, trying to decide if a new life started with going off script.

"The Dyme Letters. That's Beau. People write to me on the website all the time. Well, they think they are writing to me and they think I am answering them, but it is Beau. When he started writing the Letters, he really got into our movement. Got dedicated. The Letters were a way for thousands of people to get to know the new me. Beau likes sounding like a professor, or a psychologist, and my supporters love it and feel more connected to me because they think he is me." Dyme gave a half grin and adjusted his glasses, pursed his lips and then relaxed them.

"Oh, you don't write them. Huh." Maria and Anna exchanged glances.

"No. I don't."

"You're saying the Letters created a new image of you," Anna pushed.

"Yeah. The Letters were a way to get the *new me* out there to supporters and others who are just curious. I'm sure you read that Dawn sent me books, music, and I absorbed it all like a sponge and started to change. Dawn said no one would know if I had a deep knowledge of anything. I just needed to act like it, follow the script, drop a phrase here and there. So when reporters came to the prison to interview me, I did that and cleaned up my grammar. I changed my looks and that helped change public perception too."

"Do you worry some of these people who want to 'help' you might set you up to violate your parole? Someone who might resent your fame or think you are getting rich off the backs of murdered children?" Maria asked. "Those kinds are out there, you know."

"What I do know, ma'am, is you and your kid are more relentless than any reporters I've come across. I don't know why you asked me here. I don't even know why I've put up with the two of you. But I have. I am a victim as well as those kids." Dyme's voice was edgy now, impatient and cold.

He removed his leather duster from the back of a chair and put it on, hating it now because the original ones were made of linen or canvas. His was a fraud and he hadn't even known it until that kid pointed it out to him. Leather. He would cut it up and drop the pieces into that damn pond. Give it to the ghosts.

Sabbath Dyme showed himself out of the Blue house and walked back to Connie's. Instinct told him to leave this pond today. Just keep walking. Water was his enemy element, according to a Salem psychic. He didn't listen to himself.

WHO IS DAWN DANIELS?

Dawn Daniels controls millions of dollars in AFJ's donations but just try to find anything about her *Life Before Sabbath Dyme*.

In 2009, Daniels approached reporter Nora Ritt and asked Ritt to interview her.

A win for Ritt. It would be Daniels's first interview since she married her convict and moved to Arkansas.

Daniels told Ritt that she had been living in New York City and working for an unnamed design firm and for the city in the cultural affairs department, when she became infatuated with Dyme. She didn't state her position at the design firm but implied she was an landscape architect.

Daniels also told Ritt that when she moved to Little Rock, she got a job "working as" a landscape architect. Splitting hairs here, but "working as" and "I am" are not the same.

So you know. There is a big difference between a landscape designer and a landscape architect. A landscape architect graduates from a college with a degree and has a **professional license** to practice in a state. A landscape designer is not licensed and a college degree isn't required but **design certification** can be bought by attending a seminar sponsored by a design organization. Sort of like certified yoga teachers do, or personal coaches, or home decorators.

Did Daniels throw out a few words and let the veteran reporter fill in the blanks? Did Nora Ritt fact-check?

So you know. There is a difference between a convict and an inmate. Dyme was a **convict**, a man convicted of a crime and put in prison. An **inmate** can be someone held in prison waiting for trial. Ritt chose to call Dyme an inmate. Was she unaware of the difference? Or was she trying to sway readers to think as she does? To believe Dyme is an innocent victim. Maybe she ignored the differences so that she could use the catchy title: "The Architect and the Inmate."

Daniels said she was born in West Virginia. Using CheckPeople I could not find a Dawn Daniels that had lived in West Virginia, or in New York State, or even in the state of Arkansas. I have yet to find an interview in which Daniels gives the name of her parents or says where she went to high school or college. Yes, she says she is shy and wants to remain private, and keep the focus on Dyme, but so would a person hiding something.

In 2010, Daniels gave an interview to *Politics Daily.* Daniels told that reporter she was living in New York and working as a landscape designer when she discovered Dyme.

So architect or designer? Convict or inmate? New York City or State?
Daniels said saving Dyme was her personal mission, a calling, one brought to her by the universe. She was so possessed that she abandoned her profession and her New York friends and ran down to Arkansas to marry him.

Dawn Daniels is a woman possessed.

Chapter 6

Delphi Pond - Dawn and Connie - May 18, 2013 - 3:00 p.m.

Connie Leigh Horton had started the chain of events that resulted in Dawn's disappearance in the pond when she'd returned earlier than usual from Trey's, and found Dawn and Sabbath at home.

Dawn had been lying in a lounger, sunning on the deck while writing in her journal. Sabbath had been out on the pond in the canoe, fishing. The pond was red with mud from all the rain. Connie surprised Dawn when she walked out the sliding glass door with a bottle of Patron, two handblown shot glasses, and a couple of beers. While Sabbath had been in prison, this had been their habit, hers and Dawn's. Dawn hadn't thought about their ritual, how it had simply disappeared.

"Hey, girl." Connie handed Dawn a glass, poured in a shot, they clinked and threw back the tequila. Just like they had every evening for two years. Before Sabbath got out. That was how they measured time now. Before Sab was out. After Sab was out. "We haven't done this in a long time. I've missed it."

"I'm so glad you feel that way. I do too." Dawn smiled and licked a drop of the Patron off of her upper lip.

Connie poured again and they threw back another. "I needed that." Connie let out a burp then removed her black silk blouse and dropped it on the deck. Next went the AA bra, the filmy pants, the red thong.

She slowly lowered herself into the hot tub water without taking her eyes off Dawn, flirting with her.

"What brings you home so early?" Dawn asked as she felt a tingle of anxiety enter her awareness at the look on Connie's face. It wasn't the flirting, Connie flirted with men and women, it was something else, but she couldn't identify what her instincts were sensing.

Connie didn't seem to hear the question. She sipped her beer and stared out at the water. "Look at Sab out there. Has he ever caught a fish? Maybe I should ask my friend at Game and Fish to stock my pond." It wasn't really her personal pond. The four home owners around it owned it in common but since the pond touched Connie's property, she considered it hers, as she did with anything she wanted.

Dawn laid her journal, the one given to her by Anna Blue that past Christmas, on the round glass side table and excused herself for the bathroom. Connie waited a beat and reached a long arm out of the tub and stretched her manicured nails toward the book inching it toward her. She took a quick peek and slipped it back before Dawn returned. Dawn used this journal as a way to sort out her thoughts. She was adding up the pros and cons of leaving Little Rock using a journaling technique called clustering. She put a word or phrase in the middle of the page. As words came to her she placed them around the center word like the numbers on a clock. Then as second and third layers of words sprang out of her subconscious, she placed them in outer rings.

She often drew lines between the words and the result looked something like a spiderweb. In the process of clustering, her mind cleared, and her hand automatically wrote what was in her subconscious. She freewrote until she felt her inner critic on her shoulder and then she stopped, often not finishing the sentence. Once the critic showed up, it was over.

What Connie had seen was the web of words and the first few sentences. She saw enough to realize that Dawn was planning to leave Little Rock soon, was looking for a place to rent on the East Coast, near the ocean, and was considering how to break the news to Sabbath. Connie couldn't tell if Dawn planned for Sabbath to go with her or not.

Connie was both pleased and disturbed by what she'd read. She didn't need Dawn anymore for promoting the cause which was now focused on exoneration for Dyme. What she did not want was for Sabbath to follow Dawn when she left. These thoughts stirred a nervousness in her, so she tossed back another shot of tequila.

Connie sank deeper into the hot water and let her mind wander toward a plan. How to break them up and keep Sabbath in Little Rock was on her mind. She couldn't turn loose of him just yet. He might be her last fling with a young man. She was over fifty—even though she thought she looked great, with her clothes on anyway. Her thighs, not so much. Men liked her thick dark brown hair and brown eyes when she chose to make them suggestive. As a plan formed in her mind, she felt a displacement of water and it jarred her into the present.

Dawn sat down on the edge of the Jacuzzi. She had helped Connie select this model. It could hold six and the jets were strong and well placed, good for getting a stiff body going in the morning or relaxing one weary from too much gardening. It was just the two of them who used the tub before Sabbath came and then he often joined them.

"Oh! I was zoned out." Connie had been thinking about her plan, which she'd had only a few minutes to form, so she jumped a little as she opened her eyes. Maybe she was feeling guilty about what she wanted to do, but probably not. She couldn't remember feeling guilty for over a minute or two about anything, so if she had felt that useless emotion, it had passed.

Connie was thinking about telling Dawn that Sabbath was sleeping around on her. Maybe it was the combination of hot water, Patron, and beer that allowed the words to come out of her thoughts and find their way to her tongue because she heard herself speaking them before she had fully formulated her plan.

"I think you should know that Sabbath is having an affair." Connie felt her whole body go cold as she heard her own voice.

Dawn Daniels thought she was a having an auditory hallucination until the words settled into her mind. It took a moment for her to speak. "What? Sab's having an affair?"

Connie's hands came out of the hot water and flapped on each side of her face in a windshield wiper type motion. "Oh, oh." She made a little move with her eyes to the left, then an arch to the right, and gave a little oops with her mouth. "I thought you would want to know. Needed to know. I didn't mean for it to come out like that. I was trying to think of a way to break it to you. I'm sorry I was so blunt."

"How can you tell a woman her husband is cheating on her and not upset her?"

Dawn scooted over to her favorite jet and put her sore calf against it. She'd pulled it moving the end of a cross tie in the greenhouse a few days earlier. Connie had thought it would be good for Sabbath to get in touch with the earth through gardening, so she'd had Cantrell Gardens come out and construct a greenhouse. Dawn thought it was a stupid idea since Sabbath didn't really care for nature but she had not given her opinion. It was Connie's money and her house.

Connie's mouth went on overdrive. "I know you and Sab don't sleep together. I mean, have sex. You sleep but no sex—"

"Sabbath told you that we don't have sex? He said that to you?" Dawn kept her voice calm, controlled, but she was shocked Sab would tell anyone about their arrangement.

"No. I mean—sort of. One night he needed to talk. It just came out."

"He needed to talk to you about what? Our marriage or his girl-friend or what?" Dawn felt her voice rise.

"About your arrangement. That's all."

Dawn waited for more of an answer. She watched Connie's chest slowly rise and fall, breathing deep.

"Um. He told Beau about this Latina girl who goes to the university, a political science major, I think. She works at the Starbucks by the ath-letic club," Connie rambled. "He was feeling guilty and told Beau, and well, Beau told me. Sab doesn't know that I know."

"So Beau told you that Sab told him that we don't sleep together and that is his reason for cheating on me? Is that what you are saying, Connie?" Dawn pivoted around and stepped out of the tub. She dried her legs and applied lotion, feeling a stubble of growth.

Dawn sensed Connie was hiding something, she noticed Connie subtly shift so that she was no longer facing her. Ventral denial was a sign of discomfort. Dawn made it a priority to study body lan-guage. She knew Connie well after two years of living alone with her. When she was either hiding something or felt uneasy, Connie didn't face a person directly, she showed her side. She held her mouth a little tighter than usual. Her jaw, a weak one at best, became more clenched.

When she was telling an outright lie, she faced a person full on and kept her eyes locked on the individual. When she went on a twenty-five-mile bike ride, she would say fifty. She lied about where she went to college, the profitability of her restaurant. When she went to California, she talked about her great surfing, most of which was spent sitting on the board, flirting with the instructor. It didn't matter what it was, how insignificant, Connie embellished or dodged the truth or just made things up with no twinge of conscience. Yet Connie's body showed she was uncomfortable.

"Sab's stuck close to me since his release. He even calls me on the cell when we are separated in a department store. I don't believe it."

"I don't know. Beau told me and I thought you would want to know. Maybe it is just a flirting thing. Not a real affair." Connie stretched her arms behind her back and clasped her fingers together, trying to release her growing tension.

"I go in Starbucks several times a week. I've never seen any Latina girls working there. If he is fucking someone at Starbucks, they must be doing it in the restroom. I don't see when he has enough alone time to have an affair." Dawn let a little anger flare and watched for the effect on Connie.

Connie wanted to get off the topic immediately. She needed time to think. That had been so stupid, saying the bit about a Latina. She chastised herself for being too elaborate with the lie, being specific about the girl's description and told herself to shut up. Her nerves were singing and she kept saying to herself, *Keep quiet, keep quiet, keep quiet,* like a mantra. The silence lasted a long while it seemed. Connie usually liked to fill silence. Now she couldn't trust her tongue.

"I just can't believe he is cheating on me. I suppose after all those years being locked up with men, he would want to wrap his arms around some young girl, feel her tight body, no wrinkles or sags. I'm probably a dinosaur to him. Twelve years is a lot of years. I wonder if Dr. Phil has even addressed this. I bet it's normal," Dawn said with a lightness in her voice, trying to defuse the building tension.

Connie wanted to say, *You don't know him if you think that.* Instead she reached for the Patron and then hesitated and drew her hand back. Maybe not.

"You don't look, well...upset. I would be pissed, Dawn. After all you have done for him and he betrays you? You probably ought to go visit your parents and let him fend for himself for a while. Let him feel the pain." Connie raised her voice in indignation about the betrayal.

She felt disappointment that Dawn was taking this news calmly, even making a joke.

"I guess I'm in shock. That's a good idea about getting away for a while. Thanks. You're a good friend." Dawn leaned over and kissed Connie lightly on the lips. She felt Connie withdraw slightly, physical distancing, another sign of discomfort. "Think I'll go for a walk and clear my mind."

Dawn Daniels needed to sort out her thoughts and make a plan. Since writing to Sabbath in prison, and for every day after, Dawn had been in charge of the Sabbath Dyme Show. She was the writer and director, and planned to keep it that way. She needed quiet to figure out how she to handle this betrayal wrinkle.

Dawn walked along the dam road, thinking of her mother and grandmother. She wished they were alive. She was so much like both of them. She had MB now, her friend for nearly fifteen years, and that gave her comfort. She sat down on the wide wooden bench on the west bank of the pond and called MB to tell her what had happened. While they were talking Gene Walters's call came in, but she let it go to voicemail. She wanted to talk to him too, only later.

After their conversation, Dawn laid down on her back on the bench cushion and used her breathing to take her heart rate down to a dozen beats a minute, until she was again at that day.

Twelve-year-old Dawn hadn't known what she was looking at, at first, the early morning light coming in through the dining room window at a slant made it hard to see. As usual she'd gotten up before her parents and gone into the kitchen to bring them the coffee the automatic maker produced every morning at six-thirty.

Her eyes couldn't focus right when she saw it hanging there in the middle of the dining room. The round oak table where the family of three ate all their meals was not in the center of the room. It had been moved a little off to the side.

A shapeless form was hanging there in the center of the room, attached to the light fixture by a rope. Dawn didn't know who it was at first because of the hood, a pillowcase, covering the head. She stood there seeing and unseeing until she recognized the shoes and then the pants. She still couldn't see the face due to the pillowcase, but she knew. Dawn ran upstairs and shook her mother awake.

Laura, her mother, took one look and screamed. Then she went silent and calm. She brought over a dining chair, stood on the upholstered seat, and untied the rope, slowly lowering the body. Never said a word. She undid it real slow and when she was finished she simply said, "Thirteen loops," and nothing more. In that moment, life as they both understood it had ended.

The Martins owned a boutique hotel on the square in the Fayetteville, North Carolina, historic district. The hotel and other properties around it had been in the family for several generations on her father's side. Dawn had grown up in the penthouse.

The town was surprised when Laura Martin closed the hotel and reopened it as upscale apartments for single professionals. She kept the lobby and restaurant as they had been. The change was a smart thing for her to do. Dawn's mother had grown up in a rooming house near the Cape Fear River that her own widowed mother owned and so this type of setup came natural to her.

Laura kept a carved walnut box with brass strap hinges on the mahogany chest in the lobby of the building. The box had belonged to her mother and it had been displayed on a chest in the hallway of her rooming house. The top had a slit, for dollar bills or coins. Laura put a handwritten card in front of the box that read, "Worthy Cause."

Laura managed the apartments and the restaurant. This gave her the opportunity to promote her worthy causes to the businessmen who favored the restaurant for lunch. The causes changed from time to time. She had learned from her own mother it was critical to know when to walk away.

Laura put other boxes with handwritten notes all over town, at the hardware store, drugstore, grocery store, and so on. Dawn's mother generated interest in them by sending notices to the newspaper about the person in need and where people could donate. She kept a generous percentage of the donations for herself.

Dawn continued the tradition in her own way. In her sophomore year, the students in advanced business were given the assignment of creating a business, making a plan, marketing it, and so on. Dawn made her project a nonprofit organization and outlined various ways to promote the cause and got an A for her effort. Inspired, Dawn set up an information desk in the lobby and began working on her own worthy cause. At the end of the school year her mother decided to move to Florida.

A thunk in the middle of her chest startled Dawn out of her deep relaxation and her eyes shot open. A squirrel had dislodged a twig and it had fallen and hit her chest. She sat up, clearing her head as she watched Sabbath in the canoe with his fishing pole. His whole relationship with that pond was strange.

Dawn didn't like the pond, she liked free water, moving water. She loved the ocean. She had never felt comfortable with the pond, all those dead trees waiting to grab anyone who fell in. Like those turtles that sunned on the logs. She'd seen them silently slip under the baby ducks and pull them underwater by their feet, one by one, until ten out of twelve were gone, eaten. They constantly nipped at the swans' feet. On the surface the pond appeared peaceful but beneath that illusion, it was a liquid jungle, life and death. There was hardly a day that went by that Dawn didn't wish she could live someplace else. But for the time, living with Connie was her only option. When the news had come that Sabbath and the other man were going to be released on a plea agreement, Dawn never imagined she would return to live on the pond.

After Dyme's release from Varner, he and Dawn took a private jet to Seattle and then New York, then some Hollywood producers brought them to New Zealand. Their life had been full of adventures. Dawn was becoming a recognizable personality herself. She was a little uneasy with the attention she got in the latest *New York Times Magazine,* a full page close-up shot of her kissing Sab on his cheek. The writer did a great job of describing his childlike wonder and her efforts to educate and civilize him, just what Dawn had hoped to get across. The photographer had removed a few of her wrinkles too. Now they were living here on Delphi Pond, in Connie Horton's house, sleeping in her master suite, and he was in a canoe, fishing in a pond that didn't have fish.

Dyme had come to Little Rock with Dawn to do a promotion for the AFJ to raise money for the pardon, which became known as The Exoneration. They were scheduled to fly out immediately after the event. Instead, Sabbath announced he needed a time-out from the excitement to find his real self.

Dawn tried to reason with him. "Maybe it's my fault. I've pushed you a little too hard trying to get you caught up. All the museums and art galleries I've dragged you through. I won't do that anymore. Let's get a vacation rental in Mexico and chill for a while down there. Not here."

Dyme responded he only wanted to stay in Little Rock until winter was over, and Connie had said they could move in with her. Now it was spring and it didn't look like Sabbath wanted to go anyplace.

Dawn motioned for Sabbath to row toward her. "I'm going for a walk and then to yoga. You going to be out here awhile?"

Dyme looked toward the west. "Thought I'd drive out to Pinnacle and hike up the back side. Change my routine. Stir up the spirits on the mountain."

"Good idea. Connie is home, sweetie. See you later." Dawn waved him a goodbye.

It was just a short walk from the pond through the woods to the L.R. Athletic Club where Dawn figured she'd find Beau Bowen, Connie's ex-husband. The same woods surrounded the homes around the pond, the club, the Westside apartments, the small strip shopping center with the Starbucks the three of them frequented, and stretched all the way to Pankey Town and beyond.

At the club, Dawn went to the pool first and then to the indoor track where she waited for Beau to pass by the entrance. Eventually, he showed, just as she had expected he would.

"Dawn. What's wrong? Has something happened?" Beau was the kind of man a woman could spill her troubles to. He liked drama. Connie had once said she thought he had ovaries because he was so sensitive. As he put his big hands on Dawn's shoulders, Beau's face was the definition of concern.

"I need to talk to you. Can we meet after you're finished?"

"Let's go sit outside." He led her toward the gazebo. She liked the feel of his arm strong around her waist. They sat at the round tile table near the pool. Beau went to the concession window and brought back a couple of Arizona teas.

She waited for Beau to ask her a question. When he didn't, she blurted out, "Connie told me you told her Sabbath is sleeping with a college student."

"What the hell!" Beau came up out of his chair, all six foot six of him, and banged his fist on the tiled tabletop. He punched the top a couple of more times and then sucked his now bleeding knuckles. "That liar."

Dawn was glad there were only a couple of teenage girls sitting around, they looked in their direction and then they went on with whatever girls that age talked about.

"She told me. This afternoon. Less than an hour ago," said Dawn.

"God. I'm sorry. I don't know what to say, or to think."

Dawn imagined the first thought that popped into Beau's mind was, *That bitch has made a fool of me again.*

"I never told her anything of the sort. I'm not surprised she tried to hurt you though. She has a history of fucking her friends' husbands or their boyfriends. You've been her best friend for a few years. She arranged it so that I became friends with Sabbath and then she has a fling with him. It was inevitable."

"Wait, are you telling me that *Connie* is sleeping with Sabbath?" Dawn allowed shock to register on her face as her fair skin flushed.

"That's my guess. Connie put a blockade between me and my dreams. Now she's done it to you and Sabbath. It's her way. Connie gets attracted to someone and she has to have him, or her, has to possess. Once they are hers, she destroys them. People who once loved her, like I did, like you do, eventually come to despise her."

"You mean she said Sabbath was fucking a college girl to put a wedge between us?"

"Exactly about the wedge. *But,* you can be sure it is Connie who is fucking him, not a college student. She wants you to know he is fooling around except she doesn't want you to know it is with her. She would worry about revenge. Connie likes to take her pound of flesh so she assumes you would want to get even with her."

"That's manipulative even for Connie."

"Before I married her, I had dreams. The summer I met Connie I was training for the Ironman at the YMCA. It used to be across the street from this club. I even quit work at Jackson Cookie and went to work at the Ragin' Cajun as a waiter so I could put more time into training. Then Connie walked into my life. No, she stalked me, ingratiated herself to me, worked me, fooled me, used me, and I came back for more. Yeah."

Dawn listened. He seemed to want to talk, and she let him tell her what she already knew.

"I thought I understood people. Connie is in another category. When I look back, I blame being tired from all the training as the reason I didn't spot her for what she is, a predator."

Dawn had heard the story about that summer Beau met Connie. When he swam in the outdoor fifty meter pool, he set out a wide mouth mason jar at the end of his lane that had the word "Donations" written on the front. He seeded it with dollar bills. The manager didn't mind, he liked Beau. The YMCA touted itself as a place to help your dreams come true. It had a good gymnastics team and their swim team rivaled the athletic club's. Beau had donated his time helping the Y swimmers who couldn't afford pricey private coaching.

"She took the Y away from me. It was my hood. Those were my people. I had history. Mother taught swimming there when my father was in the pool business and serviced the indoor and outdoor pools.

"Mothers who dropped their kids off at the Y for gymnastics started hanging around the fifty meter pool, and I made friends with several of them. That was how Connie found out about me. She is so competitive. She was a whole lot older than those women and not nearly as good looking so she had to show them."

Connie had heard about Beau from some of her female lunch customers at Trey's and from women in her tai chi class. She was not an athlete. She did a little biking, some swimming, walked a couple of days a week. She did enough exercise to keep her thighs from going to dough, which they tended to do. She didn't have the underlying musculature of an athlete. Connie kept her weight down and wore the right clothes to make the most of what of what nature had given her.

"Looking back, I saw that Connie made it a point to come across me on the running trail. She would ask my advice on the type of new bike she should get, her swim stroke, her running shoes. She worked on the periphery, coming at me from all directions. She said she needed my advice and I admit, I liked that. I especially like the complimentary meals and drinks at Trey's. That went a long way.

"But when Connie tried to persuade me to train at the athletic club, I told her no. I was loyal and I couldn't afford the dues. She didn't push. She waited until summer ended and the outdoor pool closed for the season and then surprised me with a paid-in-full year membership at her club. When I left the Y, I left my people behind and it wasn't long before I missed what I'd had there. The jar wasn't welcome at the athletic club."

Beau took a long drink from his can of green tea. Dawn thought he was finished with his remembering, but he wasn't.

"Then, Connie wanted to get married. I wasn't excited about the idea. I'd already been married once, so had she. I finally gave in, went against my instincts, and we eloped. Boy, was her daddy pissed. He called me a loser. I heard him say she ought to marry someone who could take care of her for a change, and it hurt my feelings. I felt like I had to prove myself to him. I did qualify for the Ironman. Running in the heat got the better of me. I fainted. That was more proof to Connie's dad I was a loser."

Dawn had heard it all before, more than once. Connie had told her about her first husband, Tommy, who had been the star athlete at Hall High School. She had taken him away from Martha Graves, the homecoming queen and captain of the cheerleading squad, who was now working at Walmart. After five years, Connie had grown bored with Tommy and had a little fling with the yardman. Tommy couldn't handle it when he found them together. But unlike Beau, Tommy went after his dream. He went to graduate school and then received his PhD in geriatrics. He'd married a successful businesswoman from a wealthy family. Tommy had started his own business in geriatric counseling and she'd kept on with her own work.

Dawn liked Beau. She knew his ego had taken a big hit when he opened the door to the storage room at Trey's and found Connie fucking the young illegal Mexican dishwasher on the sacks of rice. It had been worse when he learned they had been lovers for six months. Beau and Connie divorced. He got half of Trey's instead of half her house. She had made the stupid mistake of putting him on the deed. He should have let her dad buy him out, but Beau didn't want to let Mr. Horton have his way. Dawn was aware that he regretted that streak of stubbornness. If he had sold to Connie's dad, he would have bought his freedom from her. He could have gotten his master's and his PhD. Another thing he could have but did not do, and he regretted it. He was angry with himself.

Dawn wondered, now, like she had many times before, why was he always followed Connie around like a lap dog. He devoted himself to the Dyme cause because of her. Of all things, at this moment, Dawn thought about Beau's donation jar. After they married, Connie ridiculed him about it. Life hadn't been the same since he threw it away. Dawn understood that.

After his divorce from Connie, and at a weekend retreat of meditation, Beau finally realized the symbolism of the jar. It held his dreams, and he had thrown it away because she'd laughed. He told Dawn that he still grieved over the jar like it was a dead pet. He acknowledged that underneath the positive attitudes he showed the public, he was a bitter man. He wanted to shake the negativity but couldn't seem to stop himself from falling into self-pity or break free from Connie.

Beau closed his eyes and turned his face to the left. His voice came soft, sad. "Connie's a dream destroyer. You know, I wanted to be a sports psychologist. She was on board with that when we got married. Then I was accepted to an out-of-state program and would have to be gone. That was when she turned against the idea. Said Trey's needed me, she needed me, she put so much pressure on me that I put it off and never got back to it. I know that's my fault, I learned that in AA, but..." He didn't finish.

Several minutes of silence followed before Beau opened his eyes and spoke again. "Tell me down to the detail what happened." Beau moved his chair and faced Dawn. He took her hands into his. Dawn was glad to tell Beau what had happened. He listened without interruption.

Dawn felt a whole lot better after her session with Beau. He really should have become a therapist. She made quick call to MB and then walked to the club locker room, changed into her yoga clothes, and went to the studio for a session of Bikram. She had a hard time concentrating. The words "pound of flesh" kept coming into her mind. Beau had said Connie had enemies and that she worried about retaliation. MB had asked her if she was going walk away from the marriage. MB wanted to fly to Little Rock and take Dawn back to New Orleans with her. She was a rock steady best friend. Sabbath and Connie didn't know about MB and MB didn't know about her lover Gene Walters. The heated room and the challenge of the Bikram practice finally did its work and brought the cleansing sweat and mental and physical focus she needed.

While Dawn was in yoga class, Beau trotted off toward the jogging trail that wove through the woods. He took a left at the wild magnolia tree off the main trail and stepped on the path that led to the back of Connie's house. The talk with Dawn had stirred up his resentments. Beau could admit to himself that he didn't have the guts to go after his dream and he was still angry. With every step he took along the path, he felt his fury grow hotter. He once thought that over time it would subside but it had been only been dormant, and now he was on fire with it. The AA meetings hadn't helped. He'd been in and out of the program for years, but his commitment to a higher power, to sobriety, fluctuated with his weight. Right now, he was in the program, almost in, but he still smoked weed and threw down the occasional vodka when he worked the bar at Trey's.

Beau stopped at the end of the trail and stood still, collecting his thoughts. He saw Dyme's and Connie's cars were gone. The house would be empty. He walked up the stairs two at a time, took the spare key out from under the copper planter, and walked into the house like he had when he lived there. He stood in the center of the collection she loved, the things that defined her, her objects, her legacy.

He thought how the past creates the present. How you bring a stranger into your life and she determines your future. By bringing Dawn Daniels home to live with her, Connie herself had generated the opportunity for him to finally get revenge. Who would have imagined, when the wife of a convicted killed arrived at Delphi Pond, the impact she would have on Connie Horton and the things she treasured. He smiled as he picked up the largest of the pre-Columbian bowls and threw it against the wall.

Chapter 7

Delphi Pond - Fight Night - May 18, 2013 - 6:15 p.m.

T he universe was still taking care of Dawn, or maybe it was the Bikram hot yoga. She felt settled and centered and full of plans after the class. While in a place of calm, she walked into the house and was glad to find it empty of Connie and Sabbath, who was probably still waiting for Pinnacle Mountain to speak to him.

She entered the living room, stopped, and let her eyes take in the room as it was in this minute in time, allowed herself to remember the first time she'd seen it. Every interior aspect of the house, especially the living-dining room, had been designed to impress the visitor with handmade cabinetry that housed a vast collection of antiquities, curiosities, contemporary artwork, and sculpture. *More a museum than a home* had been her first thought, *excessive need to define oneself with objects*, the second.

Dawn had known every article in the collection before she stepped into the house that first day Connie brought her. She'd prepared. The best way to get to Connie's heart was to admire her stuff. Dawn, in an earlier version of her life, had worked in Chicago for several years at an art auction house and she knew exactly what she was looking at in Connie's front room. The collection was valuable, although much of it was not in mint condition and wouldn't satisfy a serious collector. The pieces had been collected by Connie's grandparents, not Connie. She was the beneficiary, not a true collector.

Dawn laid it on thick. "What a beautifully aged leather wingback. Is that a Sheraton? And the companion tea table, that must be a Sheraton also. Oh, I don't believe it. A Robsjohn-Gibbings chair in a wonderful shade of lemon. The reupholster is excellent." She took her time wandering through the room, commenting here and there.

Connie was pleased and a little intimidated. She could speak with very little authority about most of her things; she knew only enough to appear as an expert to the uneducated. What seemed to be important to her was that people were impressed. Dawn saw this area as The Bragging Room and Connie more as a hoarder than a collector. Dawn respected collectors who took the time to educate themselves, appreciate, respect, and love the objects they accumulated.

On this night, the vengeful side of her smiled as her eyes roamed around the room, seeing it in shambles, destroyed, humiliated, murdered by someone who really hated Connie Horton. The art lover, the true collector in Dawn, was overcome with a sadness for the loss. She hadn't expected Beau would destroy these pieces of history and for that she was sorry.

Dawn looked to the ceiling fearing she would find the Calder mobile cut into pieces, but it still hung in place, floating above the room, seventy-two inches of metal pieces that weighed less than two pounds, worth two million dollars. Connie had bought it to replace the one she thought her father had left her in his trust but hadn't. She had used AFJ donations but claimed it as her own. Dawn knew the history of that particular Calder, something Connie hadn't bothered to learn. She had located the mobile while Connie was searching the internet for one. Although Connie thought it was her search efforts that found the Calder, it was Dawn that made the purchase possible through her connections with collectors and art dealers. Dawn speed-dialed MB to ask for another favor as she ran down the steps to the storage shed to gather what she needed and make some arrangements.

Dawn had barely finished her work when she saw the lights of Dyme's car coming down the drive. She ran upstairs to the master suite, turned on the shower, stripped down, and soaped up. She stood under the hot water, channeling her inner actor, the spirit of her maternal grandmother, the strength of her own mother, going over in her mind multiple scenarios that could play out in any direction.

Sabbath stepped into the living room and froze. He didn't know what he was seeing. It looked like a tornado hit the place and it stank of bleach. He hated that smell. It reminded him of prison. He gazed at the destruction before it struck him that an intruder could still be in the house, and he called out for Dawn as he ran upstairs toward the bedroom.

Sabbath jerked open the shower door. "Are you okay? What's happened here? The house?" His face showed alarm.

It was the sight of him standing there looking at her naked with concern on his face that brought her completely into the present where she needed to be.

Dawn lunged toward him, pushing him backward. "I just found out you are having sex with a college girl. Do I look okay with that, Sabbath? Do I?"

"What?"

"Get out of here. I want to get dressed. I'll let you know when I'm ready to talk. Out." Dawn pushed him out of the combination bath and dressing room area. She pulled on a pair of panties, a bra, and reached for her black wrap dress hanging on a hook and stepped into a pair of loafers.

Dyme was sitting on the bed when she walked into the bedroom. He stood up and came toward her. "What's going on, Dawn?"

"Are you having some kind of physical contact with a college girl?" She got up in his face and poked her finger in his chest, continuing her interrogation as if she'd not taken a break to get dressed.

"I don't know what you are talking about, Dawn."

"Answer me! Who are you cheating on me with?" Her voice was lower than he'd ever heard it. It reminded him of a cop's voice.

"I'm not cheating." His body turned a little to the side as he said it. The nervous lip chewing started.

"You are a liar. Who is it?"

Sabbath dropped his gaze to his feet. "It's Connie. Me and Connie."

Dawn laughed. "Come on, Sabbath. You don't expect me to believe that, do you? More likely, you tried to fuck her, but she would not. Quit the lies."

"I'm telling the truth. I can explain. She came on to me. I didn't go after her. She started it soon as we moved in. I was scared to turn her down. I felt like I owed it to her, owed her a debt, because she helped get me free. I felt obligated and she was really persistent."

Dawn snorted. "God, you are stupid. Connie would not do that to me. We are a team. Tell me this, if she is so important to you that you felt obligated to fuck her, then why would you rat on her now? Why not just give me any name? Make up a situation. I know what a good actor you are."

"I told you the truth. Connie seduced me."

"Shut up! You are not going to destroy my friendship with Connie."

Sabbath and Dawn had reached a place in their marriage where they slept in the bed together without cuddling or even touching. An invisible force field separated them. When she edged a toe over and touched his leg, it moved away even when he was snoring.

"I did have sex with her. I did, but it's not what you think. I was practicing on her so when we finally have sex I will be good at it." As soon as he said it, Dyme knew it was a mistake.

"You fucking liar! That is the craziest thing I've ever heard. Why not practice on me, your wife, the one who worked to save your sorry ass? Just say you find me repulsive. Tell me you would rather sleep with your mother than me. Because that is how old Connie is. No, older than your mother, one year older than your toothless mother."

Her right hand went up and she slashed him across the cheek with her fingernails. Three streaks of blood immediately rose to the surface of his soft white skin. She could feel his skin under her nails. Skin to skin, finally a physical intimacy.

Dyme raised his hand to hit her. He stopped himself. His eyes fell on Dawn's metal computer case. He was a little jealous of the computer and how she paid more attention to it than she did him. Dyme grabbed it off the dresser and heaved it across the room. It went through the open glass sliding door, across the deck, and fell into the pond. He immediately wished he hadn't done that.

Dawn howled and flew at him with her fists. Dyme looked into her eyes and saw only what he thought was pure craziness. Maybe she was having some type of nervous breakdown. Maybe it was menopause. Hormones or whatever caused it had driven her mad.

"How dare you lie to me," Dawn screamed over and over as she pounded his chest until he couldn't take it anymore.

He hadn't realized the strength in her fists. She looked so soft but her hands were rock hard and her hitting power was knocking the breath out of him.

Quick as a flash, Dyme grabbed her wrists to stop her attack. It took more strength than he thought, and he had to do it a couple of times, making marks on her wrists. He gave her a shove to get her away, she fell over the antique footstool that once belonged to Connie's grandmother. He hated that little stool, covered in that stupid prissy material, it was an obstacle to trip him at night when he went to the bathroom, that's how he saw it.

Dawn crawled across the deck and pulled herself up on the bench, sat on it, and then stood. Her whole body shook and he could see that if she stepped back one more step, the rail would hit her in the back of the knees and over she would go.

"Dawn. Get off the bench. Now! You are going to fall. Get down."

"So you can shove me around some more? No way. Get away from me." She took off her loafers and threw them at him, then waved her arms as if to shoo him away. The motion caused a little instability in her balance.

Dyme saw the potential for disaster and reached to grab her, to save her. She stepped back from the safety of his outstretched hand. In that moment of dynamic tension between falling and not falling, Dawn locked eyes with Dyme. He thought she looked serene, accepting, like he would imagine a person would when death was inevitable. Then she was gone into the dark and muddy water of Delphi Pond.

Chapter 8

Delphi Pond - Anna Blue - May 18, 2013 - 9:00 p.m.

Anna Blue stood on the balcony in front of her bedroom and peered through her binoculars into the bedroom of the house across the pond. When she was a kid she had called the binoculars her "truth seeking goggles." A senior at Pulaski Academy now, she had been studying for a chemistry exam when loud shouts from Connie Horton's house on the west bank of the pond came blowing her way. Anna lived on the east side and had spied on all of her neighbors for as long as she could remember. She stood behind her screen of potted plants that lined the front and the sides of the deck off her bedroom. The bushy plants provided her a place to hide while she watched.

Connie Horton's bedroom was the subject of her attention this night and had been most of the time since the famous Sabbath Dyme moved in. Connie lived in a pole house. Her upstairs bedroom at the front of the house cantilevered over the water. When Dawn and Sabbath moved in, Connie had given the couple her room, and she took the guest room in the back of the house. This was lucky for Anna because the fight, physical and loud, was taking place in the suite, and she had a clear view through her binoculars. Anna had been diligently recording events at Connie's house since Dyme arrived. It made a nice change from watching Connie Horton with her boyfriends.

She set her truth seeking goggles in one of the pots and jotted notes in her handmade journal. She had designed six of them for herself and ordered them from Blurb, paying for them with her babysitting money.

Anna couldn't decide if she wanted to be a journalist or work at the CIA. She figured she would make a good spy since she was only five feet tall. She had hoped to grow taller but that didn't happen. Most people tended to look right over her head. She felt her outstanding feature, besides her mind, was her big bright blue eyes. Anna noticed everything and had a photographic memory for numbers. The one thing she knew for sure was one day she would write a book about the weirdos that lived around the pond.

The pond itself was a living entity. It had history. It had known death. It contained human bones. Many years ago, in the twentieth century, before Little Rock spread west, the pond had been a swamp known as Devil's Hollow. In the early1950s, an old woman named Frederica Pike who owned a hotel in town, bought the swamp and a hundred acres adjoining it and turned the swamp into a pond. She put up a short rock wall along Highway 10, the northern boundary of her property, and set a bronze plaque into the native stone. The plaque read *Delphi*. Frederica stocked the pond with fish. Then the turtles came, followed by snakes, beavers, and waterfowl.

For a while the black congregation of a church whose members lived in a settlement known as Pankey Town, just down the highway from the pond, used it for baptisms until their minister fell in and drowned. The police had to drain it to find his body. It had snagged on one of the many submerged rotting trees that had once thrived in the swamp.

As Little Rock moved west out Highway 10, also called Cantrell Road, businesses and shopping centers came, along with subdivisions, leaving Delphi Pond and the four houses that surrounded it as a kind of anachronistic oasis. Anna lived in one of the houses with her parents. Connie Horton lived across from Anna, and to the south Dr. Billy Wade and his family, and next to them Ron Cole and his wife, Lisa.

Until Sabbath Dyme came, Ron Cole had been Anna's main focus. After the military, Ron worked as a civil engineer until a motorcycle accident cracked his skull open. He worked part time after the accident. Occasionally, he would have crazy spells his wife called "the troubles" because they always caused a lot of trouble for her.

Like the crazy spell he had on the day of Anna's eighth birthday party when Cole got on his dirt bike and rode through the woods naked. He flew through the party, took down the pink Barbie tent, and nearly ran over the clown doing a magic trick. The bike headed down the embankment toward the pond, hit a beaver dam, and Ron Cole went airborne over the bars. The girls heard him scream, "Goddamn beavers," before his body hit the water. He sank and didn't come back up.

Good thing for Cole, Dr. Billy saw him land. The birthday party ran toward the spot too. When Dr. Billy pulled Ron out, there was a piece of a tree sticking all the way through his thigh. Maybe it was a bone. The girls screamed and ran toward the house. Anna pulled out her pink cell and punched 911. After Cole got home from the hospital, he was calmer. The doctors had adjusted his nervous pills and that left him less emotionally messed up. Without his dirt bike, he didn't have a way to burn his pent-up energy. Ron wore his brown hair clipped short to the point of looking bald. A jagged scar ran from his left eyebrow up the top of his forehead, across the top of his skull. Ron still had a swimmer's build with long thigh bones, big feet, broad shoulders. At the gym in his house, he'd gotten as muscular and tough as he had been when he was a Navy Seal, but the part of his brain that controlled reasonable behavior still needed some healing.

Cole had built a four foot high natural stone fence along the periphery of his acre to keep the "damn ducks" out. They roosted on it. He patrolled the pond and the woods surrounding Delphi Pond wearing a gun belt like a cowboy and in it was a .45 revolver. He said it was for the water moccasins, but Anna had seen him put his wife's cat in a plastic bag, knot the top, throw it into the water, and use the bag for target practice until it sank.

There used to be a pair of swans until the male pecked at Ron and he shot it. Anna had seen these things when she had been stalking him and taking pictures. Now a death a row killer had moved to the pond and Anna was watching him and his wife fight. She wondered if Ron Cole was on patrol this evening.

Anna took her camera bag and tripod off a shelf in her office. It wasn't really an office. It was supposed to be a second bedroom for the baby that never came. When the third round of fertility treatments didn't work, Maria had an opening cut between the rooms and Anna took over the space and used it as a playhouse. Now it was her office. It had a small refrigerator like the kind in a hotel, and a desk, and shelves for her hobbies.

Over her desk was a picture of her second grade class that Maria had enlarged to poster size. It showed Anna standing in the front row, a head shorter than her classmates, her blond hair hanging to her waist, and her eyes looking toward the right—not at the camera. Her smile was more of a grin, a grin that would one day be described as a "shit-eating grin." Under the picture, Anna had written, *What matters is how smart you are, not how tall.*

Anna attached the telephoto to the camera. When Dawn ripped the gash in Dyme's cheek with her fingernails, a thought popped into Anna's mind, *She has his DNA under her nails.* Anna figured they were fighting about sex.

Anna wondered if Dawn, who was usually soft spoken and calm, had found out Dyme was having sex with Connie, or maybe being married to an ex-con wasn't as much fun as she had hoped. Anna had spent quite a bit of time with Dawn before Dyme came. Sometimes Anna and Ron Cole helped Dawn create rock gardens in the yard. Dr. Billy had stitched up her finger at his house when she cut herself on a broken piece of glass. Dawn brought flowers from the garden to Maria and Lisa. The pond people liked Dawn although no one knew her well.

While Anna attached the camera to the tripod, a commotion occurred across the pond. A splash. The ducks and geese protested with honks and flaps. She pointed the telephoto down to the spot on the water where the spotlight from Connie's deck shone and saw Dawn's case bouncing on the dark water. Anna knew that she kept her laptop in it.

The silver case hung in the pool of light from the outdoor floodlights before the current took it toward the spillway. Little Rock was having the wettest spring in its history, the most violent and numerous thunderstorms, and the pond was running swift. Water poured over the concrete spillway. It created a little waterfall. Knowing the pond all her life, Anna figured the case would end up caught under the big oak that made a bridge across the creek that the spillway's water had created in the woods.

Anna heard Dawn's shouts and imagined it was the sound a mom would make if her kid fell in the pond. She went at Dyme with her fists, screamed and hit him in the face and chest. He stood there at first and did nothing, just took it. Then fast as a whip snap, his hands flew up and circled her wrists, grabbing her once, twice. Then he gave her a shove backward. She stumbled and went down hard on her butt. Dawn crawled out on the deck and pulled herself up on the bench next to the rail, she stood on it, her back to the pond.

Dyme was directly in front of Dawn and Anna couldn't see him well. She could see Dawn's back, her standing on the bench, the rail a little lower than the back of her knees. She stood on the bench like a woman who saw a snake, or a big spider, or a rat in the room and was trying to get to high ground and away from it. When she threw her shoes at Dyme, Anna selected *continuous* on the camera and squeezed the shutter release. The Nikon snapped off shots as gravity took Dawn Daniels backward over the rail into the dark water where she disappeared.

Chapter 9

Delphi Pond - Searching for Dawn

The Blues, Coles, and Dr. Billy went looking for Dawn as soon as Maria alerted them to what had happened. Ron directed the hunt and he had them spread out along the east and south ends of the pond. Ron took the area on the west side. He had a good idea where to look. Cole walked along the narrow drive on top of the dam, his light tracing a pattern across the asphalt. The dam road was part of Horton's long private drive that started at the highway entrance of her property, ran under the pole house, and ended at Butterfield Lane. Butterfield met Peck Road which ended at the highway.

In Ron's opinion, Connie's drive was an open conduit to anyone who wanted to rob or rape her and get away with it. He had tried to get her to secure her place, especially the road, with cameras, fencing, and gates. Connie told him that security of the kind Cole recommended was way too expensive for her pocketbook. Connie did have an alarm system installed in the house but it kept going off at all the wrong times so she quit the service and left the sign in the yard and the little security boxes on the windows and doors. She nailed no trespassing signs on trees at the Highway 10 and Butterfield entrances to her drive.

Ron figured that Dawn landed in the deep water next to the dam. He could smell duck shit from all their nesting places along the bank. He heard the fowl honking and flapping, scattering, away from him as he inspected the area, finding only her computer case. She did not get out of the water there.

Ron knew Dawn could hold her breath for at least two minutes. Anna had told him that she had seen Dawn swim underwater for fifty yards at the athletic club pool. Anna said she was impressed because Dawn was over forty and could swim that distance underwater, without a breath, while she was on the swim team and thirty yards was her max. Being a former Seal, and knowing Dawn's underwater swimming skill, Cole thought she would play it safe, take off her dress, let it go, and stroke her way underwater toward the unlit center of the pond. She would come up, take a look, and carefully make her way to the north end of the pond swimming underwater, coming up for a quick breath, and continue that pattern until she reached the shore near the highway. That was the only thing that made sense to him since no one had seen her.

Cole walked along the dam road, looking out toward the center of the pond, his eyes accustomed to searching in darkness. When he saw her head break the surface and quickly duck under, he went to the area close to Highway 10 where he assumed she would get out. He waited there and when he saw Dawn wobble out onto the bank dressed in underwear, he only stood still and watched as she crouched low and hugged her arms close to her body. She crawled toward a low stand of bushes and curled up beneath them. He didn't know if she was hiding or trying to catch her breath. She'd been in the water about twenty minutes. Dawn jerked as Ron came up behind her and touched her foot. She bolted up and ran toward the highway.

Cole caught her by the leg and brought her down, dropping the computer as he lunged. She fought like a badger until she realized who had her and then collapsed in tears. He covered her with his vest and held her shivering body. He pulled out the flask from his hip pocket and told her to take a few slugs to warm herself, which she did.

"Let's get you to my house and have Dr. Billy take a look at you," Ron said. Dawn objected.

"No! Look, I know the police are going to be careful about Dyme. Those lawyers of his will paint me as crazy, and Connie will help. I have to get the attention of everyone or I will never be safe. Forget you saw me. Please. This is my only chance to get away from him. Please."

It didn't really matter to Ron Cole. Dawn Daniels had come to live in his territory and no one entered his domain without his checking them out. It was his duty to protect the pond. Cole had friends in the private security industry, he had Dawn Daniels's fingerprints, and that was about all they had needed to find out who had been living with Connie Horton. He had kept what he had learned to himself, like he did most things. As a special forces man, he knew loose talk could compromise a mission. Keeping quiet became a habit, a way of life he still practiced. Ron thought life was safer when people didn't know what you knew.

"I never saw you. Go! Now!"

Ron watched Dawn run toward the highway as if she were running from the devil. A car skidded when the driver slammed on the brakes to avoid hitting the crazed figure coming toward it. The driver, an elderly woman, got out on wobbly legs and collapsed. An oncoming car nicked the front fender of the stopped car and a man got out, cell phone in his hand. He checked the women, took several pictures with his phone, made a call, then went back to his car and brought out a couple of beach towels and covered them. A woman with an iPhone videoed the scene while they awaited the paramedics.

A fire truck from the station less than a mile away arrived first then the ambulances and the police. Ron had already joined the Blues and Dr. Billy by the time the sirens cut through the air. None of them seemed to notice they hadn't seen him for a while.

Chapter 10

Delphi Pond - Detective Bill Brass - May 18, 2013 - 10:30 p.m.

L ittle Rock Police Department Detective Bill Brass pulled up to the Horton house. He'd gotten a call from Chief of Police Marshall Knight. He and Brass had attended the same college and had been roommates for three years. They liked the same kind of beer and weapons. Chief Knight hired Brass five years earlier. Brass had been a detective in Denver for nearly twenty years when he quit, needing a change. Brass knew who Sabbath Dyme was and didn't have the same strong opinions about the ex-con as many of the local police did. That's why Knight called him in on the case. Sabbath Dyme's wife was in the emergency room at St. Vincent. She was accusing her husband of attempted murder. Brass sent his partner, a young female detective, to the hospital and he drove out to West Little Rock to see Dyme.

Brass looked around the property and found the front door open. He stepped inside. The front room had been vandalized. Brass drew his weapon and checked the house. Empty. Malicious damage and assault at the same house on the same day? Too much of a coincidence. If something was missing that would make a coincidence even more unlikely.

Brass started down the steps and saw Ron Cole walking toward the house. Ron wore what looked like a pair of pajama pants or scrubs, like surgeons and people who wanted other people to think they were doctors wore, and a sleeveless tank.

Brass knew Cole from the shooting range. They were both competitors at the same club, and they'd had beers together after practice several times. Cole was an excellent shot. He ought to be; he practiced every day. Brass had been to Cole's house once to see his gun collection and it was impressive. Some pieces dated back to the eighteenth century. He knew guys like Cole, who'd never gotten over their special forces days. They carried a special kind of burden. Although Brass sensed the man's troubles, he liked Ron Cole.

Cole came to the foot of the steps and called out, "Hey, Brass. What's a hotshot detective like you doing down here investigating a break-in?"

"Hey, Ron. Do you know anything about what happened here?"

"Nope. Dawn came running over to my place saying someone had broken in. She wanted me to check out the house with her. Boy! Someone did a number on it. No one was in there, and I told her to call the cops. Is that cop you?"

"Seen Sabbath Dyme around?"

"No."

"You must know something."

"Not much. We all heard the yellin' from Connie's place. Anna saw him push Dawn over the rail. Maria called me and Dr. Billy, and Anna called 911. We came out here looking for her. Then we heard the sirens and the ambulances out on the highway. We went to see what was going on. Dawn was lying on the road. Someone else was there on the ground too."

"Did anyone question you or the neighbors?"

"No. When the ambulance left, we all came back home."

"Dawn Daniels accused Sabbath Dyme of attempted murder."

"Whoa! I predicted when they let him out that it wouldn't be long before he got himself in trouble. You out here to arrest him?"

"Don't know if there has been a crime. I wanted to have a talk with him, but he's not here. Think I'll have a look around. You know this place. Walk with me."

"Not unless you force me. I've had enough of this insane night. I need to have a conversation with a couple of shots of bourbon."

Cole turned and walked back toward his house.

Brass checked out the exterior of the property. He walked the bank along the creek and found a silver case bobbing against the trunk of a fallen tree and picked it up. He then saw the drag marks coming out of the creek and followed them. He located the shed. The door was locked. He reached above the frame searching for a key—people hid their keys in the most obvious places—found it, and opened the door to find a hog-tied Dyme.

"Are you really here?" moaned Dyme.

Brass took one look at the gash in Dyme's forehead and called for an ambulance. He snapped pictures with his cell and then cut him loose and told him to remain still. Which wasn't necessary since Dyme was so stiff his arms and legs were useless and didn't feel like they belonged to him any longer.

"Who locked you in the shed?"

"I don't know. Some hunter dude. Big guy dressed in hunting gear. Had a mask over his face."

"What happened?"

"I was looking for Dawn. She fell off the deck. I was following that creek and he came up behind me. He had Dawn's case. I tried to get it from him and he hit me and the next thing I remember is being in the shed."

"What did he hit you with?"

"I don't know. A gun, I think. He did have a gun, I'm sure of that."

"What did he look like?"

"Tall. He was covered up with camo clothes. His face, all of him. It was dark and I could barely see him at all. He stayed behind me, mostly."

"What else did he say to you?"

"Nothing."

"Does anything about him stand out in your mind? His voice, speech patterns, things like that." Brass didn't like where his intuition was headed.

"I can't think. My head is splitting."

"Hang on. I hear a siren."

After the ambulance carried Dyme away, Brass walked toward along the shore to the Blue home. He passed the Cole and Wade houses and could see into every window that faced the pond.

Brass studied the house Richard Blue and his wife lived in with their daughter, Anna. The pathway to the house consisted of a series of ascending six by six foot cedar decks lighted from beneath. Maria Blue met him at the door with her husband. Brass introduced himself and they invited him inside. A young girl stood up and greeted him, Brass figured she was about fourteen or fifteen and was surprised to learn Anna had just turned seventeen.

Anna Blue took in all six foot four of Brass. He towered over her and her parents. The detective wore his Levi's tight and his dark hair was cut short which made his green eyes stand out. He walked like an athlete and had the no-nonsense look of a person used to concentrating. His face wrinkled in the places a face does when a smile is real. Anna thought he looked more like a football coach than a police detective.

"How's Dawn?" Anna asked right away. "We saw the ambulance. Looked like she was hit by a car."

"She's in the ER right now. I don't know her condition."

Brass turned to Maria and Richard and asked for their permission to question Anna. They sat around the kitchen table and Maria served hot herbal tea.

"What about Sabbath? He didn't look conscious. Who beat him up? Did you find him? Did you arrest him?"

"Anna, enough." Maria touched her daughter's hand in a settle down motion.

Brass knew Richard Blue was a lawyer and an accountant who specialized in construction contracts and litigation. He'd also come across Maria in a courtroom once or twice.

"So, Anna, what did you see tonight?"

"How do you know I saw anything?"

"I listened to the nine eleven call. You made it."

Anna paused and looked at her mother before she answered, giving Brass an abbreviated version of events. He needed clarification and walked her back through it.

"You heard loud voices. Why did that alarm you?"

"They were fighting, yelling. That was unusual and I was curious. I wanted to see what was going on." Her mother said she had to tell the whole truth and not delete a thing, so Anna admitted she had been watching Sabbath Dyme since he came to live at Connie's.

"Why did you take pictures?"

"I just wanted to see what the camera would pick up. Photography is one of my hobbies. You want to take a look at the photos?"

"Yes, I'd like that."

Anna loaded them into preview and turned the screen in his direction. Brass studied them. Richard didn't move. He kept quiet. He didn't step in or act like Brass thought a lawyer would. He let his wife handle it.

"You can tell the difference between someone who fell and someone who was pushed?" Maria Blue asked him as she looked over her daughter's shoulder.

"We have experts who can tell." He studied each of the pictures for several minutes.

"I saw you put Dawn's case in your car. Did you open it?" asked Anna.

"Why? Is there something in it I need to see?"

"I don't know. Just wondered. She went crazy when he threw it out the door and she has it with her all the time." Anna glanced in her mother's direction and Brass caught it. So did her father.

"Mrs. Blue, I'm trying to understand what happened. This is a serious situation for Dyme and a delicate one for our department. I don't have evidence that he did or did not assault his wife. We just have the accusation of a wounded and upset spouse. If Anna can help, we would greatly appreciate it."

Richard finally spoke. "Excuse us, Detective, I'd like to speak with my family in private." He gestured toward the balcony door.

Brass stood looking across the pond at the Horton house. He didn't need binoculars to see in every window facing the pond. What looked like windows were a series of ten foot sliding glass doors. To his left were Ron Cole's house and Dr. Billy Wade's. Their houses, like the Blue and Horton houses, were wide open to the pond.

Brass watched Ron Cole lying back in a recliner, the TV flickering. Dr. Billy was standing in front of an open refrigerator drinking out of a carton, not wearing a thing. The other three sides of the houses were surrounded by woods, giving the illusion of privacy. Brass couldn't live with his flank exposed like that and wondered how they did, especially Ron Cole.

"Detective Brass," said Richard.

Brass turned toward Anna's father who had reentered the room alone.

"I've talked to my daughter. She doesn't have any information that will help you other than the photos. This is all the help we can give." He handed Brass the flash drive.

Brass thanked him.

"Do you have children, Detective?"

Brass said he did not and while they chatted, car lights appeared on the driveway to Connie Horton's house.

"Looks like Connie's home," Richard said.

"One more question, if you don't mind. When you and the neighbors were looking for Ms. Daniels did you see anyone else around the property?"

"No. We split up. I'm sure Maria or Anna didn't or I would know about it. Maybe Ron or Dr. Billy might have seen someone."

Brass left and quickly walked back to the Horton house and found a concealed place from which to observe. He watched Connie react to the crime scene tape he had put across the steps to her entrance. He saw her bend and pick up the card he'd left there and then his cell rang.

He answered. "Brass. I'll be there in a few minutes, Ms. Horton," and hung up without giving her a chance to speak.

Brass called into the station. He wanted that computer case retrieved from his car immediately and examined thoroughly. Something vital was in there, he was sure of that.

Chapter 11

Delphi Pond - Brass Interviews Horton - May 18, 2013 - 11:30 p.m.

It was close to eleven-thirty p.m. when Connie Horton returned home. She paced next to her white Nissan Pathfinder, cell in left hand, right gesturing along with her words.

Brass heard the rise and fall of her excited voice as he made his way toward her. When he reached her car, she ended the call and got up in his face, this tall, pear shaped woman, whose breath smelled faintly sour.

"What the hell is going on? Where is Sabbath? What have you done with him?"

"I don't know—" He was going to say *which hospital.*

Horton interrupted. "You don't know where he is or you don't know what's going on? I will tell you what I do know and that is you can't keep me out of my own house." She gestured toward the yellow crime scene tape across the handrails of the stairway leading up to the front door of her cedar pole house. The steep stairs ran up twelve feet to the first story of the two story house with decks that cantilevered over the pond.

Brass kept his features neutral as Horton ranted about police abuse of private citizens' rights with such volume it brought Dr. Billy, Ron Cole, and the entire Blue family out onto their decks.

Connie Horton wore long black wide-legged pants with a deep purple oriental style jacket, her dark hair pulled back tight against her small skull with a jeweled clip. The pitch and range of her voice, the dramatic gesturing with her arms, the push of her head toward him and then the pull back of it away from him reminded Brass of a Kabuki play or maybe a puppet show. The exterior floodlights illuminated her performance. It was all way over the top.

Brass fixated on her jaw. How she kept it clenched while she ranted. The movement of her jaw was so stiff, it seemed as though it had once been wired shut. What movement took place came from her shapeless red lips that worked back and forth, spitting her words out. Connie's big brown eyes and perfectly arched eyebrows were not enough of a distraction to keep his eyes away from her teeth.

Brass wondered why this obviously vain woman—he judged her vain from the expensive designer clothes she wore and the apparel in her closet as well as the high end furnishings in her home—had not done anything about her teeth. Not only were they crooked, their laminates had turned a light gray. Teeth were fixable with implants or caps, orthodontics, whitening solutions, even jawlines could be adjusted to fit the face. Connie Horton needed a talented cosmetic dentist and that was what Brass was thinking about when he realized she had finally shut up. The night was wonderfully silent, and the silence hung in the air.

Connie, who didn't like silence, picked up her rant again.

"Look. I don't have to talk to you unless I want to and I am not sure that I do. I know about Dawn supposedly falling off the deck. Dr. Billy told me, and I know about the 911 call and Dawn ending up in the ER and calling the police. I've heard all of that nonsense about Sabbath pushing her."

She tore the yellow tape off the rails, balled it up, and threw it at him. Brass caught it as it left her hand.

"Why are you here?" She emphasized each word as she stomped up the steps. Brass followed. He was going to say something but didn't. Her world was about to collapse.

"Oh god! Oh god! Oh god!" Connie's screams rang out across the pond into every house around it, sounding as if they came from within the very framework of her home.

Horton's cell rang. She didn't have sense enough to answer, having collapsed on the floor in a heap looking like a deflated purple and black balloon. Brass looked at the caller ID. Dr. Billy. Using his own cell, he called the number, introduced himself, and asked the doctor to let the neighbors know there was nothing to worry about. Brass waited for Connie Horton to recover herself. He went out on the deck where there was a telescope. It was not pointed toward the stars.

Connie lay in a heap in the middle of what was once her collection of artworks, antiquities, and curiosities. Wall hangings centuries old had been turned white with bleach, ancient pottery smashed and pulverized into dust, the spines of rare books broken and the pages shredded. It was murder of sorts and committed by a person eaten up with hate for this woman. Brass could feel it as surely as she did. Or maybe she didn't feel it, the hate, all she was feeling right now was pain.

After a long while, a diminished Connie picked herself up off the floor and ran to the bathroom. He heard her retches, the toilet flush, the shower go on. She emerged wearing a long floral silk bathrobe, her wet hair loose around her shoulders. She opened the door of a hand-crafted liquor cabinet, withdrew a fifth of expensive brandy, and poured herself a snifter full. For Connie it was brandy for comfort, tequila for excitement, gin for anger, pot for sex, and Ambien for sleep.

"Would you like a beer?"

Brass declined.

Connie pulled up a bar stool, sat with her back to the destroyed room, and sipped her brandy. She spoke without looking at him, resting her forehead in her right hand.

"I don't remember, why are you here?" She sounded exhausted.

Brass pulled out a stool with the toe of his boot, straddled it, and recounted the evening— the 911 call, Dawn's accusation of attempted murder.

"Ms. Horton, do you know who would vandalize your home?"

"You or your officers." She said it like it was a fact.

"You think police officers did this? Why?"

She looked straight ahead and spoke in a monotone. "The police hate me and Sabbath Dyme. I got him out of prison. Me, not Dawn. Me. That whole thing had stalled out until I got the community involved. I made fools out of the police. Tonight they get a call from a woman who happens to be my best friend who has lived with me for over two years and she accuses Sabbath of trying to kill her. Y'all come here hoping to arrest him. You wreck my place figuring I will think he did it and turn against him and help you put him away again."

Brass didn't comment. When she didn't break the silence he did. "Daniels's accusation is serious. She could send Dyme back to prison. The best way for you to help Sabbath is to tell me what you know."

"Right. Give you more information to twist. Forget it. I'm the victim here, and Sabbath, not Dawn."

"If you're right then he needs your help."

Horton seemed to consider this and asked again, "Would you like *anything* to drink?"

Brass accepted water. Connie told him about what had happened that afternoon.

"I came home to take a nap. I gave up my bedroom, actually it's a very large suite, to Sab and Dawn when they came back after their travels. I haven't slept well in the guest bed. I got up and found Dawn out on the deck crying. She was very emotional, said she was going home to spend time with her parents. That didn't sound like her. After a while, she confided that she'd just learned Sabbath was cheating on her with a college girl from UALR. I wasn't really surprised. He is a young man and well, Dawn is older. She asked me what I thought she should do about it, but I didn't offer any advice."

Brass had read in a recent *New York Times Magazine* article that Dawn Daniels had not left Dyme's side since he got out of prison. The report was personal, quoting passages from their letters. Dawn had stated she was working on his table manners, that he had so much to learn about cutlery. She was improving his taste in film, trying to wean him from horror movies, trying to give him some sensibility about the finer things. She said he was still a teenager in many ways. If the article was meant to show their relationship as sweet, it showed Brass that Dyme still had no life of his own. He couldn't even choose his own movies or his own eating utensil.

"Then what happened?"

"We talked awhile. Then I had to shower and go to the salon. I got the works, head to toe. I was attending a patron's party at the Arts Center, very exclusive, and didn't get back home until, well, you were here. I had my cell off all evening, and when I got your message, the first thing I did was call Dr. Billy and he told me what had gone on." Connie finished her story and the last of her brandy.

"Who do you think did this?" He gestured toward the room.

"I told you already. You or your officers."

"You are smarter than that. This level of destruction is personal."

He waited to hear her reply. She said nothing. Her eyes were locked on the ceiling, staring at a loose monofilament line dangling from the cedar beam. Then Connie Horton fainted. Brass caught her before she hit the floor and carried her to the sofa. It took longer than Brass expected for her to come around but when she did her first words were, "Robbery. I've been robbed. My Calder is gone."

Brass kept silent. He waited for the crime scene techs to arrive and for Horton to recover.

"I had a vision about evil when I was passed out. I know who did this to me. Dawn. She has erased ancient things from the face of the earth. That is evil. Humans are the only evil thing on the earth and if you didn't know it before, you are seeing it now. And she is a thief. She stole my Calder."

Brass had not expected to hear that. "Why would she do that?"

"Me. I am her motive. I think she figured out that Sabbath and I are lovers. She just said the college girl thing to me to see my reaction. Setting me up, trying to make me mistrust him."

"That is conjecture, ma'am."

"I know what I know, and I know she knows about me and Sab."

"When you left this afternoon for your appointment, was Ms. Daniels here?"

"No. I think she said she was going for a walk and then to work out at the club. It's just a five minute walk away through the woods. She could have hid in there and waited for me to leave and then come back to do this."

"Again, you are speculating."

"Somehow she found out about me and Sabbath and this was her revenge. Then she jumped off the deck and said Sab tried to kill her and that was her revenge against him."

Brass changed the subject. "What is the size of the mobile?"

Horton brought him a photograph and description of the piece. Brass thought it looked like something he could make out of coat hangers and pieces of scrap metal.

"This thing looks unmanageable for one person. It is over six feet long when stretched out and has twenty-four or so moving parts. I don't see how one person could have cut it down from that height and handled it at the same time."

"Dawn only looks helpless. She's a whole lot stronger than she seems and more athletic. All that yoga she does? You saw my rock garden. She built it, moved those rocks herself, and some by rigging things to make them roll. Shit like that. She probably rigged something up or got someone to help her steal my Calder. Besides, it is made of a lot of little pieces but it isn't heavy at all, probably two pounds, at the most."

"Are you saying she has a partner in stealing your property and wrecking your house? Who would that be?"

"I don't know. Dawn is secretive. Just Google her. There is nothing at all about her except when it comes to Sabbath. She is super secretive. Not normal. There is absolutely nothing stored on her computer except a few pictures and a couple of emails. Everything is kept on one of those secure internet sites or whatever they are called. The kind with all sorts of tricky passwords and codes and things."

"How do you know about her using these encrypted sites?"

"We've lived together two years. Sometimes, if her laptop is open, I take a peek but find nothing. Secretive, that's Dawn."

Brass thought, *Unlike you, who can't get enough publicity or information about yourself out in public.*

"Your art collection isn't a secret, Ms. Horton. You don't have any type of security system. You are open to the highway. Anyone could have stolen your property."

"Not anyone. It was Dawn. She is getting even with us, me and Sabbath. You don't think she fell off that deck, do you? If anything she jumped off."

"We have a witness who saw her fall."

"Who? Little Snoop, Anna Blue? Please. That kid's imagination is boundless. The water below the deck is deep. This house straddles a dam. My ex used to dive off it and swim across the pond and back when he lived here. Back when I was impressed that he was an Ironman."

"Have you seen Ms. Daniels jump off the deck?"

"Not off the deck, but when we went to that resort where you can swim with dolphins, she did a back dive from a diving platform. I was afraid to jump off it, but she dove backward."

Connie stood and faced Brass. She wagged her index finger in his face to emphasize her words. "Look here, Detective. I don't have to talk to you. I want you to leave. I want you to put it in the record that Dawn Daniels stole my Calder, and she vandalized my property. My word is good enough."

"There is the matter of proof, Ms. Horton. You say she had motives, but there is no evidence she knew about you and her husband and no evidence she did this to your property."

"That's your job, to find it." Connie opened the door and waited for him to leave and then slammed the door shut.

Brass returned to the shed. He'd remembered that he'd seen a few peanuts of packing material.

Chapter 12

Delphi Pond - Pond Families React - May 19, 2013 - 9:00 a.m.

The Delphi neighbors gathered at the Cole house the next morning. Ron wasn't home. He was at Connie's and something was going on over there. It was Sunday, and like they often did on Sundays, they visited with each other over coffee and donuts or scones. Anna called it their Sunday worship since none of the pond people went to church. They watched Ron carry boxes from Connie's house to the leased Subaru Dawn and Dyme shared. Connie followed him, talking at Ron nonstop.

Richard Blue asked no one in particular, "Does Dawn have any friends or family?"

"Aren't we her friends?"

"No, Anna. We are her neighbors." What he knew about Dawn came from his wife and daughter. He was still disturbed over the story Anna had told him the evening before. He wondered if his daughter needed professional help. Maybe she would grow out of it. Well, maybe not. Ron Cole was as big a snoop as Anna and he was over forty. He thought now, as he had all during the night, about the story Anna had told him concerning her investigation of Dawn Daniels.

The day of her interview with Dawn, Anna had left Connie's house and headed straight to her computer to track down MB, Morel Baptiste Bienville, from New Orleans, hoping to discover something personal about Dawn Daniels from that search. Anna found MB with little difficulty. She was a lawyer and one of the best poker players in the country. The poker playing got Anna's attention and she decided to learn the game. Bienville had a cousin named Augustus and Anna had heard of him, seen a video of him performing. He played in a rock band and was a minor celebrity in and around New Orleans. He stood on top of a tower while he played his guitar with the rest of the band below him.

Taking a break from the search, Anna picked up her binoculars and looked into Connie's living room where Dawn was now working on her laptop. Deciding she'd had enough for a while, Anna grabbed her swim bag and headed to the club. As she crossed the dam road and walked toward the path that led to the club, Dawn came out of Connie's house.

"Hi, Anna," Dawn said as she unlocked her car. "I'm off to Cantrell Gardens. Big sale." She waved a flyer. "I've got so many new ideas for the shade garden. I could spend a week in there looking around."

"Let me know if you need some help unloading," Anna offered.

"I love looking around that place. See ya."

Anna kept walking until she was deep enough that the woods hid her. She waited until she was sure Dawn had left. Anna set her bag down on the trail and went back to Connie's. She climbed the deck's trellis and pulled herself onto the deck. She had noticed the sliding glass door was a little ajar and hoped that it had stayed that way.

She found that it was and slipped inside the house. Dawn's computer case was sitting on the kitchen counter and beside it her laptop. Anna saw that Dawn had not shut it down. The screen was still opened to the file Dawn had been working on. Anna took a peek. It was the P.V. Two website. Nothing of interest there.

Anna searched through the computer files and found the only things stored on the hard drive were photographs and emails from supporters. There was nothing personal or financial, but Anna did learn that Dawn had an account with a site that provided secure off-site document storage. She could not access that site without a username and password.

The computer case was something that Dawn seemed to protect and Anna always thought that was an odd thing. She opened the metal case and felt around the padded interior. As she pulled back the egg-shell foam, she saw the corner of a drawing, and removed the padding entirely.

Anna studied the intricate drawing of a flower. It was made up of letters and numbers. Anna realized this flower was a way for Dawn to record the usernames and passwords without them being obvious. She memorized what she was looking at and took the added precaution of snapping a picture with her cell phone.

The splash on the spillway got her attention. She hadn't realize how much time had passed. The trellis was on the side opposite of where Dawn parked so Anna climbed down and went into the woods. She knew it well enough that she could make her way back to the trail to get her swim bag without being seen.

Anna walked to the club pool, changed into her suit, and sat under an umbrella. She took out her iPhone, feeling a sense of urgency mixed with excitement. She pulled up the secure site and opened an account for herself. It was then she learned that the site recorded the time and date of each access. If she got into Dawn's account there would be a record of it and Dawn would know someone had discovered it. Anna felt frustrated because she had the passwords but didn't dare enter the site. The heat and humidity began to take its toll. Anna put the phone away and eased herself into the cool water.

When Anna confessed about her break-in to Connie's house to dig up more information, she was not surprised at her dad's reaction.

"For god's sakes, Anna. Please tell me you know how wrong that was. Tell me you were not going to tell that story to Detective Brass."

"No. I wasn't. I just asked him if he opened the case."

"Why? It got his attention."

"It just came out of my mouth. I wasn't going to tell him I broke into Connie's house. I'm not stupid. I just wondered what was in the case. She went totally crazy when Dyme threw it into the pond. Her reaction was completely over the top. I thought something important might be in the case. I knew he wouldn't tell me, but I couldn't stop myself from asking."

This Sunday morning, Richard was not indulging in donuts and coffee. He was sticking to Mountain Valley Water, thinking about the previous night's confession, with one ear listening to the gossip around him.

"Do you think he really did that? Tried to kill her?" Lisa Cole rocked in her deck chair as she spoke. She hadn't slept at all either. "Richard? Are you with us?"

Richard said, "Sorry, Lisa. Did he try to kill her? Is that what you asked? Brass said experts could tell from Anna's pictures if she was pushed or not."

"I wished I'd looked at them carefully," Maria said as she passed a basket of her biscotti around.

"I saved them on my hard drive, Mom. And, I saw him push her and then he pushed her again."

"The more we stay out of this the better." Richard gave Anna and Maria one of his looks that meant business.

"It sure looked like he pushed her." Anna opened her iPad Mini.

Maria said, "I worked on a case recently that involved a memory error called misattribution of memory. That's when a person mistakes fantasy for reality. Misattribution is more common than most people realize and it really affects criminal investigations and testimony in court. I think because Dawn was under heavy stress, she had a memory about something that did not happen. A shock can cause that to happen too."

Lisa said, "There was always a little something off about her, chasing after a killer and marrying him. What kind of woman does that?"

"You've never said that before," Maria said.

"Well, maybe it's Ron, his paranoia is contagious, but there is something off. Think about it. We've had a fair amount of contact with Dawn over these years and yet know nothing about her."

They watched as Cole got into the Subaru, drove up the drive, and parked the car in his guest parking area, then locked the car and walked into his house. Connie drove away in her Pathfinder. Every one of them peppered Ron with questions when he stepped on the deck.

"Here's the story." Cole sat down and Lisa handed him an iced coffee. "Connie said Dawn stole her mobile, whatever that is, and completely tore up that collection of hers. Said there was nothing left. It was smashed, shredded, and bleach poured all over everything. Connie's gone off to meet up with her lawyer and Dyme's lawyers. That's all I know. None of you need to worry. I've called in security. They will post men around our property to keep out the damn idiots that are bound to swarm here."

Ron did not tell them that the previous evening Dawn had come to him and asked him to check the house for intruders because someone had broken in and vandalized Connie's place. He also kept to himself that Dawn also asked him to store three boxes for her. Dawn told him that she was going to confront Dyme about his cheating when he got home and that she planned to leave him. She said she had packed up the only things she cared about but he had the car and she didn't have a place to put them. He was glad to help her. He figured if Dawn left, then Dyme would leave too.

Dr. Billy, an avid antiquities collector himself, had long coveted many of the things in the Horton collection especially the pre-Columbian pottery. He put his hands over his ears when he heard "smashed and pounded into dust." Then he asked Ron, "What do you mean you put men out at the drives?"

"I told you, Billy, this is going to be a circus. There's gonna be reporters, those cult followers, pardon perverts. Who knows? Damn nuts all of them and they're going to flock here like geese. Got to keep them out. My buddy in the security business is taking care of it."

"God, Ron. When are you going to get over it? You are not in a war zone. This is not Iraq, or Iran, or any of those places. This is Little Rock, Arkansas. You're overreacting. Right, Lisa?" Dr. Billy looked to Lisa for support. She stayed neutral. This was the first she'd heard of guards and knowing Ron, they were probably armed with machine guns.

"I told you when Dawn moved in she would bring trouble and here it is, Billy. You should thank me for thinking ahead. Hell, man, you've got three little girls. You don't want to find them like he left those boys, hog-tied, dead, in a creek. He uses water to cover his tracks and there is plenty of it around here."

Dr. Billy's voice was heading toward the upper ranges where it went when he was stressed or really tired, and this day he was both. "That was graphic, Ron. What does the house look like inside? What's left? Any intact pieces of the pottery? Details, please."

When Ron finished describing the scene, Dr. Billy shook his head and finished his thought. "Dawn appreciates history, art, artifacts, she would not destroy things that are historically significant. That is not

Dawn. I tell you. It simply is not her. They are best friends. Why would she do that?"

Anna stood with both her arms in the air like a gymnast getting ready to perform. "I know the answer. I know it." She waited, looking at her dad, considering what she was going to say. "Dawn found out Connie was having sex with Sabbath."

A chorus rang out, "Anna!"

"Well, it's true. I saw them."

"Anna!" Richard looked at his wife. "Maria!" She shrugged. If Anna hadn't told her mother this, Richard wondered what else his daughter had kept to herself.

Richard said, "When did you see that? How? Never mind. Don't say a word. Maria, get rid of the binoculars."

"If it's true, how did Dawn find out? Who would have told her?" Lisa asked.

Cole said, "Let me be clear. Connie didn't tell me that she had sex with Dyme. Connie told me that Dawn asked her if she knew that Dyme was cheating on her with a UALR student. Connie told Dawn yes she knew, and that Beau had told her. Connie said that Dawn was mad at her because she didn't tell Dawn when she first heard about it. Dawn found out yesterday afternoon about the affair. That's all I know."

"Wait a minute, I'm confused," Dr. Billy said. "Are you telling us that Dawn is getting even with Connie for not telling her about Dyme's affair or because Dawn thinks Connie is sleeping with him?"

Anna interrupted. "I am still right about Connie and Sabbath. I saw them. Two times."

Cole raised his voice. "Everyone, hold on! Listen to what I am saying, folks. I'm telling you what Connie said. It isn't my speculation. It's what she said. Connie thinks Dawn busted up her place because Connie didn't tell her right away about Dyme's sleeping around. Connie thinks Dawn accused Dyme of pushing her because she wants revenge. *Anna* is the one who thinks Dawn found out that Dyme and Connie are sex partners. Little Snoop. Anna Blue. Not me, Ron. I don't know anything but what I have been told by Connie."

"I saw them, and—"

"Anna! Quiet!" Richard held up his hand. "Enough."

"Where is Dyme?" Richard asked. The last any of them knew of him was when the ambulance took him away.

"I agree with Billy," Lisa said. "Dawn didn't do it. That sounds like the work of a crazy person. Tossing one or two pieces of pottery around, maybe she would do that, but not what you've described."

Ron Cole was thinking that it all seemed pretty clear. Dyme had gone off the rails and acted like the killer he was.

"It makes me mad every time I think about how Connie and her goddamn crusade brought all this trouble to our door," Ron said.

"When was Dawn supposed to have done this? I saw her walking down the dam road but I didn't see her come back. Connie was still there and so was Dyme," Maria mused.

Anna said, "When I went over to the club for swim practice, I saw Dawn and Beau out at the gazebo together. I was going to wave but they looked so serious, I kept going. When I left the pool and went to the weight room, I saw her in the yoga studio. I can ask Shelly if Dawn stayed in class the whole time."

Richard raised his usually quiet voice. "You will not! You will stay out of this. Do you understand me, Anna? You all can sit around and play detective all you want but keep it in this room. This is not a game. This is gossip and he is a killer. You aren't going to listen to me, are you? I admit it. I can't control my wife or my child. I admit it. I am guilty. Now, I am going home."

No one else moved except Lisa who went to the kitchen and brought back more snacks and something besides coffee to drink. She was glad Richard had left. He was always the lawyer and didn't like it when conversations got out of his control.

"I wonder if Dawn was telling Beau about Dyme and Connie or about Dyme and a college girl?" Anna was thinking out loud.

"Wait. Telling him what?" Lisa asked as she circulated with the tray.

"Let's suppose that Dawn suspected Connie and Dyme and she told Beau. Maybe he wrecked the collection as a way of hurting Connie because she betrayed Dawn."

"Beau? That is pretty far-fetched," Dr. Billy protested. "He's not a violent person and why would he care what Connie did or didn't do? They're divorced. They work together. I think they patched up their differences. I can't see it."

Maria reminded them of what had happened when Beau found out Connie was sleeping with that young dishwasher who worked at their restaurant. Someone went into her house and cut the crotch out of all of her slacks and her underwear. She called the police but nothing ever came of it. They told her to change her locks, but she hadn't.

"I remember that," Cole said. "She came over here crying, over-wrought. She wanted me to go over to her house and see what had happened. I told her then she needed a fence around her property and an alarm system. She thought it was Beau that did it. I told her how to secure her place but she didn't do it."

Maria said, "Dyme told me and Anna that he and Beau had got-ten to be friends. Maybe Beau felt like the avenging angel, not just for Dawn but for himself too, for her betrayals of him in the past."

Ron said, "Hell, for all we know the vandalism was a cover, a dis-traction for the real crime. Didn't someone say that mobile thing was worth a couple of million? Whatever, that's it for me. I've had enough of this speculation. I'm going to the shooting range." Cole stood up but made no move to leave.

"So we have three suspects—the unknown intruder, Dawn, and Beau," Anna said.

Dr. Billy didn't agree. "I can't see Dawn being that devious. If he didn't push her, she wouldn't have accused him. That could put him back in jail and she knows it. She's not mean. Secretive yes, but not mean. What about whoever who put Dyme in the shed? Maybe they did it?"

Ron Cole didn't want to go down that road. The last thing he wanted was to have a brainstorming session about who was where last night.

"I'm outta here. Back in a couple of hours, Lisa." He kissed the top of her head and left them chattering away. Billy right in the middle of it all, like one of the girls.

"What I don't get is we were out there looking for Dawn and none of us saw any strangers. It seems like we would have seen someone around. Whoever did it knew the woods and the trails. I was outside all afternoon, I would have seen a car come down the drive. Maybe it was Beau. He always took that path to the club. Maybe he wrecked the house and put Dyme in the shed."

Anna broke into her mother's trail of thought. "Look at this, every-one. I enlarged the photos. I made a mistake."

They clustered around the iPad.

Anna traced Dawn's backward arc with her finger and said, "That looks like a dive to me."

The others nodded their agreement.

Chapter 13

St. Vincent Infirmary -
Brass Interviews Daniels -
May 19, 2013 - 10:00 a.m.

While the pond people were sitting around speculating, Dawn Daniels was waking up in St. Vincent Infirmary. When she arrived at the ER, Dr. John Mills contacted the police based on the word "assaulted." Mills knew Dawn from the athletic club.

Mills explained to the officer on the phone that Sabbath Dyme's wife was in his emergency room and she had accused him of assaulting her. A female detective was sent. Mills recommended overnight observation and put Dawn in a private room. He gave her something for anxiety and sleep. In the morning, when awakened by the sounds of the hospital, she felt drugged and anxious, not rested.

Dawn sat up and tucked herself in the lotus position. Putting her thumb on one side of her nostril and her middle finger between her eyebrows, she started a series of alternate breathing exercises that would allow her to relax.

This was how Detective Brass found Dawn when he entered the room, she was in the middle of the bed, her eyes were neither opened nor closed but hovered somewhere in between. He stood still and observed her. She sensed him in the room and fully opened her eyes.

"Glad I didn't scare you. I'm Detective Bill Brass, LRPD. I'd like a word."

A finger rose up to indicate he give her a minute.

Brass waited for her to speak. It took nearly five minutes. Finally, she said, "I'm a nervous wreck and my meditation practice helps me so much."

Dawn's voice was soft and her demeanor shy. She tilted her head down a little when she spoke. The tilt, the voice, the upturned eyes, gave the overall impression of a humble woman.

Dawn came by acting naturally. Her paternal grandmother had been a stage actress in New York before she married Sam Martin and moved to Fayetteville, North Carolina. From her, Dawn developed her love of costuming and taking on roles. Coached by her grandmother, she honed her natural skills as a mimic. Even as a child, she was an astute observer of a person's mannerisms and could impersonate quite well.

By the time she was five, Dawn had her own wardrobe room and by eight her grandmother had filled it with costumes, jewelry, wigs, all sorts of props. She liked to pretend she was someone else, especially after her daddy hanged himself.

In Florida, where she and her mom moved after her mother sold the apartment building and the restaurant business, Dawn worked part time for a scuba shop. Back then, she wore her long hair pulled away from her face in a single braid that reached to her waist, dressed in khaki shorts and tight tank tops. The owner never had to tell her anything twice. She worked hard on her days in the shop selling trips. She was an excellent water person. Scuba customers felt safe with her as guide, and she often amazed them by free diving to one hundred thirty feet and sometimes more.

On her days off, Dawn practiced her acting skills. Dressed in her one of her disguises she would stop by the Scuba Shack or other shops where she was known and no one recognized her. She had cosmetic dentures of the quality makeup artists used that would change the shape of her lower face, ones that could give her crooked teeth or straight teeth, big ones, little ones, stained teeth, diseased gums. She put a pebble in her shoe to give her a limp or lifts to become taller, wore designer clothes, or looked like a bag lady or a dowdy housewife or a worn-out mother, a professional woman, a bored rich lady. Wigs, she had many colors, styles, long, short, spiky, braided, clean hair, dirty hair, badly cut hair. Her fingernails could be bitten, long, dirty, manicured. And so on.

Dawn noticed Brass looked a little fatigued and that gave her the edge. Dawn had no doubt that anything she told this good-looking detective he would believe.

So when Brass asked how she was feeling and Dawn said, "Shaken." She was waiting to see the doctor. She looked at his left hand, which held her computer case, and noticed he wasn't wearing a ring. She reached toward him and Brass set the case on bed.

"You found it. Thank god. My whole life is on that computer."

That wasn't exactly the truth. Her whole financial life, and a lot more, was stored online, not on the computer itself. There wasn't any value to the case except the passwords arranged in a flower drawing hidden behind the case lining. Dawn believed in insurance. The drawing was hidden in several places not just in the case.

Brass pulled up a chair and sat next to the bed. "Dawn. Do you feel up to telling me what happened?"

"Where's Sabbath? Did you talk to him?"

"I haven't. He's at Baptist Medical."

"What happened? Was he hurt when you took him in? Did he resist?"

"We don't know his condition but it isn't serious. He had a nasty gash on his head when we found him. I don't know what happened yet."

"Did you arrest him?"

"No, ma'am. He is in the hospital. I'd like to know what happened to you last night."

Dawn had spent quite a bit of time thinking of how to tell the story of the attack. She didn't respond to him. She made him wait and ask again.

"Tell me what you remember. That's why I'm here."

"I just don't know how or where to start. Maybe, ask me a question that's not so, well, broad." Dawn released herself from the lotus position. She turned to face Brass and let her legs hang over the side of the bed.

"Okay, Ms. Daniels. Did Sabbath Dyme attack you unexpectedly?"

"Oh, no. We were fighting. He got really angry, crazy looking, and that scared me. I was afraid he was going to hit me and I ran from him. I got to the rail of the deck. I couldn't go any farther. I got up on the bench and he pushed me. I went over backward."

"What caused the fight?"

Dawn took her time telling about the "hot tub incident" as she put it and how Connie told her about Dyme's affair with a college girl. She explained her decision to confront him, how hurt and angry she was.

"You've brought me up to the time you spent at your club. What happened after you left?"

"I walked back to Connie's. We only have one car and Sabbath had taken it.

When I got there, the place was torn up and it scared me. I got Ron Cole, a neighbor, to come over to make sure no one was still in the house."

"You said this was about six-thirty. When did your husband return?"

"Oh. I don't know. The sun was just about to go down, I think. I don't really know."

"What happened after you fell?"

"After he pushed me and I hit the water, I swam to the highway end of the pond and flagged down a motorist." She did not mention being spotted by Ron Cole.

"That took some courage to swim in the dark to the far end of that pond."

"That shows you how afraid I was of him."

"Was? Are you no longer afraid?"

"I feel safe now that the police know what he did to me."

"Do you think he may have tried to grab you to keep you from falling? Maybe you were unsteady."

"I do not. He deliberately threw me off the deck like he did my case."

"Threw? I thought he pushed you?"

"Pushed. Threw. He tried to kill me. That's all I know. Maybe he didn't *plan* to kill me, but he pushed me off the deck and that is the same thing."

"No, ma'am, it isn't. If you have evidence, I need to know about it."

"He pushed me backward off of a deck, a second floor deck. I was there. It happened to me. That is attempted murder or at least assault. If he is trying to murder the one who has stuck by him all this time, then he is not stable. He is a danger. He can't control himself. He needs help. It is your job to protect the community." Dawn spoke slowly, like a fifth grade teacher explaining a new kind of math problem.

"What were you wearing when you fell?"

"When I was pushed? I had on a black wrap dress."

"What happened to it?"

"It was pulling me down so I took it off."

"That took some presence of mind."

"Detective. I lived in Florida and worked on a dive boat when I was in my late teens and early twenties. I am comfortable in the water. I was the top platform diver on my high school diving team. Working on a boat, I was trained in CPR, open water rescue. Instinctively, I knew what to do. I dropped my dress and I swam to save my life."

Dawn's instincts were zinging with the line of questioning. She felt like a suspect instead of a victim. Intuition told her Brass had broken into her secure files. She reshaped what she had planned to say.

Brass said, "Don't you think it a bit unusual for a woman to walk into a scene like you did and not call the police? You entered the house and took a shower. Why didn't you call the police?"

"Calling Ron Cole is better than calling the cops. He was in special forces and he knows the pond better than anyone. Ron cleared the house. He told me to call the police but I decided to let Connie handle it. It's her house not mine. Besides, I wondered if Sabbath and Connie got into a fight after I left and he did it."

"Why would you think that?"

"Connie and I are close. I thought maybe she confronted him about cheating on me and they argued and in a fit of temper he destroyed the collection."

"Does he have a volatile temper?"

"At times he does. Like last night. I would say he was very volatile."

"Did he take the Calder too?"

"What? I didn't even think to see if anything was missing. I didn't know it was gone. That's going to kill Connie."

"If you thought Dyme vandalized the home, would you not fear him? Why would you stay in the house?"

"I didn't *know* if he had done it. But if he did, then he was mad at Connie not me."

"Ms. Horton believes that you vandalized her home and took her Calder."

"She told you that? That's absurd! Connie and I are friends, a team. I love Connie. She's done so much for me. There is no way she believes that."

"I spoke with her last night. She stated that you found out that it was she and your husband having the affair. You came back to her home when it was empty and vandalized it, stole her Calder, and then accused your husband of assault as revenge."

Dawn's brow wrinkled in disbelief. "My husband is having sex with Connie? I don't think so..."

"Who told you about the affair between Ms. Horton and your husband?"

"This is outrageous. Now I am the culprit and they are victims? I can't comprehend why she would say such a thing—if she did."

"Did you learn that Ms. Horton and your husband are lovers?"

"No. She told me about Sabbath and a college girl."

"Ms. Daniels. Often people who have suffered a shock, such as you did, remember what they think happened instead of what did happen. Could it be that you took a step backward and accidentally fell?"

"Are you saying you believe Connie? I see now what you are. You are one of those women hating cops who blame the rape victim for getting raped, aren't you?"

"Not at all. Dawn, you were scared. I am saying you may be mistaken about what you remember. Look at these photos. A neighbor captured these images. Experts have analyzed them. Your body position is not consistent with a shove that would throw you backward off the deck twenty-four feet above the water." Brass handed her the photographs.

Dawn examined each one for a long time, all the while thinking of Anna Blue, the Little Snoop of Delphi Pond. "These are barely in focus and dark. Hard to tell what I'm seeing. What is *not consistent* supposed to mean?"

"Look at your arms." Brass explained how the various angles of her body and arms did not look like an uncontrolled fall.

"It looks to me like my instincts took over and my body was trying to control the fall. A diver would do that instinctively." Dawn looked at Brass with tears in her eyes. "Detective Brass. I am so tired. I am scared. What is it going to take for me to press charges against Sabbath? Obviously, you don't believe that he pushed me off the deck, but I don't care what some expert says. I was there. Do I have to get out of this bed with my fanny hanging out the back of this gown and go down to police headquarters and beg the chief to file charges?"

Brass kept quiet. Dawn was more than familiar with the silent treatment tactic. Most people were uncomfortable with silence and would fill it. She didn't mind silence but decided to continue speaking in the hope it would move him to her side.

"Look. Detective. I appreciate what you are trying to do, to find the truth. That is what I have been fighting for these many years. Justice for the falsely accused, justice for the murdered children. Maybe you are trying to make up for what the police and the justice system did to Sabbath. I am not falsely accusing him. If he cannot control himself with me, what will happen when someone he doesn't love makes him mad? It is my duty to see this through. Surely you understand."

Dawn's explanation of social injustice in her teacher voice set her nerves on edge. During this interview she had been a teacher, a diver, a wounded spouse, an assault victim. She was tired and had started relying on answers she'd used in interviews months earlier. That was not good and she hoped that Brass did not recognize the speech.

The door opened and a nurse walked in. She asked Brass to leave the room.

Brass stood outside the door with one leg bent, the sole of his boot against the wall. It was his habit, this waiting position of leaning against and scuffing the wall.

He took out his phone and watched the YouTube video again. It was set to the sound track of the old *Dragnet* television series and the narrator's voice had the same tone and quality as the original announcer. The scene opened with Dawn Daniels unconscious on the highway, naked, except for her bra and underpants. An old woman lay next to her. The narrator spoke: "Sabbath Dyme's wife —victim of attack."

The sights and sounds of the police and ambulances arriving and the crowd growing, and then Dawn awakening, screaming hysterically, "Sabbath tried to kill me. He tried to drown me in the pond. Someone help me, please," made for intense viewing. The medics wrapped her in a blanket and put her in the back of an ambulance. The next scene showed Delphi Pond, the water reflecting the lights of the houses around it. The *Dragnet* soundtrack concluded the video, "Dum dum dum dum-dum."

A stunning woman, tall, athletic, honey blond hair, wearing a cherry red sweater that clung to her perky breasts, white skinny jeans, and pair of heels that brought her to a little over six feet, walked toward Brass. She was hauling two shopping bags from Walmart. She removed her white island-style Maui Jim sunglasses as she drew closer. Her brown eyes were alert and intelligent. They scanned her environment as she walked, taking it all in. *Like a cop,* he thought.

Stopping in front of him she said, "Are you with Dawn's security team?" All Southern charm and batting eyelashes.

"Bill Brass. Detective. LRPD."

"Very, very pleased to make your acquaintance, sir. I am Morel Baptiste Bienville, a friend of the victim. Are you protecting her?"

Brass heard the New Orleans influence in her vocal cadence. She was playing with him but he'd never minded a good looking woman flirting with him.

"No, ma'am. I'm first in line to see Ms. Daniels when the nurse finishes."

MB didn't wait for the nurse to finish. She pushed open the door. Brass heard the excitement in Daniels's voice and turned to get a view of their greeting. MB held Dawn and smoothed her hair for a long time. Neither noticed Brass in the doorway.

"Excuse me," Brass said, entering the room. "I'll get back with you later, Ms. Daniels." He placed his card on the bedside table and left.

"Good-looking man," MB said as she handed Dawn one of her two Walmart bags. "Brought you some clothes. Let's get out of here."

"They aren't going to release me. Not with the police —"

"Haven't you learned to trust me yet?" MB held up the second bag.

When the two women left St. Vincent, MB acted the part of an old woman. She replaced her high heels with a pair of house slippers. Over her jeans and sweater, she wore a long terry-cloth robe, and covered her head with a brown scarf. Dawn looked like her caregiver, in scrubs and sturdy white shoes. She guided MB toward the waiting limo and helped her inside.

"Central Flying," MB instructed the driver.

Less than fifteen hours earlier, MB had landed the Cessna Citation Mustang at Adams Field. She had parked it at Central Flying, rented a car, and driven out to West Little Rock and left the car in the LR Athletic Club overflow across the street at the now abandoned Y. She had pulled up close to the path that ran through the woods. She followed the trail that Dawn had described to her, took a left at the wild magnolia, and entered the back of Connie Horton's property. The ground was mushy from all the rain and she was glad she'd worn boots. The place looked like snake paradise. Snakes didn't scare her. She just didn't have time to deal with a cottonmouth's bite.

MB located the wooden shed, and on the concrete floor lay the long narrow box. She picked it up and carried it like she would a surfboard back to the car. Then she drove her cargo to the UPS Store in the shopping center at Sam Peck Road and Highway 10. The owner was locking up when she pulled in. A one hundred dollar bill persuaded him to open back up. MB shipped the package to a secure storage facility in Fort Bragg, North Carolina. She drove to the downtown area, registered at the Peabody, settled in at the bar, and waited for Dawn's call.

At around eleven, MB had started to worry. She hadn't heard from Dawn and couldn't reach her by cell. The flicker on the bar television got her attention, and she nearly choked on her straight up Don Julio 70 at the breaking news.

"Sabbath Dyme's wife flees for her life." A YouTube video appeared on the screen. Dawn screaming, "Sabbath Dyme tried to kill me." "Dum dum dum dum."

MB finished her drink and went upstairs to her room. After a few calls, she found where the ambulance had taken Dawn and got a good idea of what had happened from her internet searches. She'd never known Dawn to act impulsively or do anything that would draw attention to herself. She was a person who operated according to plan.

The plan had been for Dawn to have a chat with Dyme, tell him she knew about his affair with a student and that she was going to leave him. She would pack her car and meet MB at the Peabody and the next day they would fly to New Orleans. The first game change came when Dawn asked MB to pick up a package and ship it for her. Now there was another change of plan that MB didn't know a thing about and that worried her.

MB took a hot shower and went to bed. She couldn't sleep for thinking about Dawn Daniels, the woman she met nearly fifteen years earlier. When they'd met, Dawn Daniels was known as Lauren Martin and MB had just graduated from law school.

Chapter 14

Central Flying Service -
May 19, 2013 - 11:30 a.m.

The Flight Deck at Central Flying Service bills itself as "Home of the Greatest Cheeseburger in Aviation History," or so the menu read. MB began to relax for the first time since landing in Little Rock. The restaurant overlooked the runways and MB liked watching takeoffs and landings. She had logged about twenty hours of helicopter training and watched a Robinson R4 take off. MB decided she would buy one to train in. Maybe an R2 would be better for a beginner since it was smaller. While Dawn was in the restroom, MB looked up the price. Not bad. MB felt hungry enough to eat two of the greatest cheeseburgers. She held back, and requested one with an order of home cut fries and a tea and ordered the same for Dawn.

"Here." MB handed her friend the *Arkansas Democrat-Gazette* when she sat down. "Read all about your evening."

Below the fold, a shot of Dawn Daniels being loaded into an ambulance. The headline read, " 'Sabbath Dyme tried to kill me.' " Dawn read the article.

"MB, did you take this picture?"

"I was at the Peabody waiting for you to call me. I even turned down a poker game. That's my degree of devotion, sweetie. That picture came off a YouTube video. Here look at it." She pulled it up on her iPad.

Dawn watched. "Some random person with a smart phone put this together. Definitely a Dyme hater." Dawn had a fantasy that it had been Ron Cole but she didn't know how tech savvy he was.

"This is a big problem for Dyme, but you don't look like you care."

"I don't give a rat's ass. He was fucking Connie. We worked together twenty-four seven to get his sorry ass out, and they fuck each other. That is another way of saying 'Fuck you for all the work you have done.' I say the gods took this video, and Dyme is getting what he deserves and so will she." She kept her voice angry.

MB tried to keep her voice neutral since Dawn's was filled emotion. "Okay. The last we talked, you wanted me to fly here, pick you up, mail a package, and meet you after you had a heart-to-heart with Dyme. What happened?"

"He told me he was having an affair with Connie, and I went a little crazy. I really did. I was mad at both of them, but he was the one in front of me so he got the brunt of it. I slashed him across his face with my nails and then he came at me. I was genuinely afraid of him—for the first time ever. He threw my computer case in the water and grabbed me by my wrists. He twisted my arms. See. Bruises.

"Anyway. I got up on the deck bench. I had a sudden inspiration. I felt like I was on a high dive. When he came toward me again, I let myself fall backward. I just relaxed and went with it. The only thing is that fuckin' Little Snoop across the pond was spying on me and took pictures. She gave the pictures to the cop, Brass. If it wasn't for those photos, his skinny white ass would be headed for Varner right now. I figured a way to get around that complication, but I am not sure if Brass bought it."

MB held up a hand. "Let me get caught up. You were going to tell him you knew about the affair with the student and that you understood. You were going to tell him you were leaving him? No fuss. It was just the end of this chapter in his life. When he told you about Connie, you lost your temper and the result was the fall, rather dive. Is that correct?"

"Yes. And another thing. I swam toward the road and got out. That damn Ron Cole was looking for me, all the neighbors were, because of that Blue kid. Cole grabbed me. He wanted to take me to Dr. Billy for a checkup. I told him I was scared of Dyme and was going to run to the road. I told him I wanted the attention of some passerby who would call the cops and that would protect me. He didn't give a shit and let me go. As far as I can tell he didn't tell Brass. He hates Dyme. I do know that. So I don't think Cole is a problem."

"Okay, but now you want to put Dyme back in prison?"

"You bet I do. He is a betrayer. He deserves it. I bet he really killed those boys and this is the universe's way of putting him back where he belongs."

"Okay. He cheated on you. That isn't a crime. Why, after all this work, do you want to destroy what you've done? Why put him back?"

"Are you taking up for him?" Her voice raised in anger.

"Lauren—Dawn. Keep it down. No. I am saying cheating is not something a man goes to prison for. That's all."

"Well, we really don't know if he killed those boys. Anyway, he betrayed me. I'm taking him down along with that cunt Connie. The IRS is going to love looking into her finances. And the Calder mobile she bought with the donations, how is she going to explain that? She has accused me of stealing it, and vandalizing her house. Did you know that?"

"I heard that along with her accusation you are getting revenge for Dyme's cheating."

"I will be avenged for their betrayal. That's true. I plan to download the complete financial records of AFJ and send them to that reporter who has been after full disclosure for so long, and to the attorney general, to everyone who has shown an interest."

"Honey, don't go down this road. You will get your revenge on Connie with those financials but leave Dyme alone. When you cool down you might regret putting him back in prison. If you are even able to, that is."

"Able to? He is a convicted killer. He was released with time served and a ten-year suspended sentence. He's violated parole by attacking me. It's a no-brainer. They will lock him up."

"Don't be so sure. There is no one to corroborate your claims. They may have evidence that he didn't push you, if I heard you right about the photos. They have Connie accusing you of revenge over their affair. I advise you to talk to Brass. Tell him you were wrong. Walk away. Otherwise you are opening yourself up to potential discovery about your past. Do you want that?"

"So what? I haven't broken the law. I am simply a super saleswoman working a Worthy Cause. People voluntarily give. If anyone gets dinged for the AFJ expenses it will be Connie."

"None of this makes sense, Dawn. I don't get your anger. Is there something going on you are not telling me?"

"MB! Don't pull the lawyer shtick on me. Listen to yourself; you're even calling me Dawn. You have never met Sabbath Dyme or Connie the Cunt. I've been on the ground here for years dealing with these people. Do you think I liked playing the role of Dutiful Dawn, walking behind Dyme, looking at him like I adored him, wearing all those cheap clothes, kissing Connie's ass because she knew the right people, building the Great Wall of China around her friggin' spillway to create that shade garden she wanted. All of that I did for the Worthy Cause and look what I got. Betrayed."

"Da—Lauren. Dyme was your Worthy Cause and your Crusade. You were successful. I urge you. Walk away and savor your victory. This is an ugly business. This is not you. You are smarter than this."

"Well, it is me now. I am staying here and seeing the ordeal through. This is personal. I don't expect you to cover me on this. I don't want that. I will get in touch when I am finished here."

"Where is the justice in putting a man in prison for cheating on his wife?"

"MB, this is the last thing I am going to say on the subject. No one except Dyme knows if he killed those boys. I am going to get my revenge for this betrayal and that is that. If you feel uncomfortable, go down to the French Quarter and have a psychic experience or whatever people like you do."

"No need to get hostile. I'm trying to help you think clearly. You are like the spy who has been undercover too long, living a lie so deep she doesn't know who she is anymore. I am afraid for you."

"MB, I'm just...just tired."

"Is there anything I can say that would convince you to walk away from this mess?"

"What I can't figure out, MB, is why you care if Dyme goes back to prison or not. You've never indicated in any way you thought he was innocent."

"Sweetie, it's you I'm worried about. Have you considered Brass might find some evidence that will lead him to the postal shop? The size and shape of the box would fit the Calder that Connie has accused you of stealing and he's obligated to investigate. He will follow that lead to the storage unit. He will know that it is yours. He will try to find who shipped it for you. He will dig and dig into your past. Trust me, I know the type. That man is a badger."

"I hope he does follow his nose. I think he has already figured out my name isn't Dawn Daniels. I caught the scent when he was in my room. He had my computer case. I am sure he knows some things about me."

"So the Calder is not in the box, is that right? What is in it?"

"Grandmother's Japanese woodblocks. You know the ones."

"The same ones you had at the Carrollton apartment? Why did you want me to mail them?"

"They are my lucky charms. Superstitious. Sentimental. That's me. Sabbath had the car. I couldn't pack up before he came back. So I put them in your capable hands. I didn't want to drag them to New Orleans and have to move them again so I had you send them to my storage unit. I see now. You thought I took the Calder, didn't you?"

"Yes."

"I wouldn't ask you to do anything that could get you in trouble. You know that."

"I guess I didn't. I thought the mobile was in the box, and I did ship it for you. Where is the Calder?"

"I have no idea. I didn't even know it was gone until Brass told me this morning. I hope that Brass does go to my storage unit thinking I have the Calder. He will wish he hadn't and I'd like that. He's an ass."

MB looked down at her submariner Rolex, her lucky charm, and the best thing about her charm, it was portable. "I've got to check the weather and file my flight plan. What are you going to do?"

"I need some money. I don't have a nickel on me. I need a car, and a cell, and then I'm not sure. I will keep you posted. Try not to judge me about Sabbath. He isn't your concern."

MB handed her friend several one-hundred-dollar bills and a debit card. "I care about *you*, Lauren, not him. I am afraid that you are the one who is going to get hurt, not him. I am in your corner and think I've proved that."

"I know you are and I thank you. Now get going. I will be in touch."

Chapter 15

Baptist Medical Center -
Brass Interviews Dyme -
May 19, 2013 - 11:00 a.m.

For security reasons, Sabbath Dyme spent the night in a private room at Baptist Medical Center. The ER doctor had diagnosed him with a mild concussion, put sixteen stitches in the side of his forehead, and cleaned the gash in his cheek. The next morning, Detective Brass, file folders in hand, found Dyme in sunglasses, sitting in a chair looking out the window.

Dyme heard him enter and spoke with his back turned. "Looking out a glass that's not barred. Figure it's the last time in my lifetime. I know how it goes for guys like me."

"You probably do. How are you feeling?"

"This is surreal. I've depended on Dawn for so long, and now she's turned on me. I didn't try to kill her. I didn't. I wouldn't. I tried to keep her from falling." Dyme hung his head, took his sunglasses off, and massaged his temples with his fingers. Brass waited, wondering if Dyme was going to try to be a Johnny Depp look-alike the rest of his life.

"You here to arrest me?"

"Why do you think that?"

"Who is going to believe me? I saw that bit on YouTube. That stupid music. Dawn laid out on the highway. Her accusation. I'm toast."

"I want to hear your side."

In spite of his lawyers warning him not to speak, Dyme told Brass about coming home and finding the house a wreck. He told about the fight, and how he'd tried to reach for Dawn when she got on the bench to keep her from falling, how he looked for her around the pond and in the woods. He told Brass again about the crazy hunter who knocked him out and locked him in the shed. And when Brass asked what his relationship with Horton was, Dyme told him they were having sex and how it got started. He let it flow, something he'd never been allowed to do since hooking up with Dawn. It felt good to just talk.

"Did Dawn know about you and Connie?"

"No. The fight started because Connie told her I was getting it on with some college girl. I denied it because I wasn't. Finally, I told her it was Connie. She called me a liar. She said I was evil, and Connie would never do that. That's when she really went at me."

"Exactly how close are Connie and Dawn?"

"They were together all the time until I got out and we started traveling. When we were on the road, they were always talking on the phone and figuring out ways to bring in money for the pardon, that stuff."

"What time did you leave Delphi that afternoon and when did you come back?"

"I left Connie's about an hour or so after I saw Dawn take off on her walk. I don't wear a watch. I think I got home by eight or a little earlier, it was dark but just barely."

Brass handed Dyme a folder. "Take a look at these."

Dyme looked at the eight by ten photographs.

Brass asked, "What's your impression?"

Dyme hesitated. "My first thought? I don't have one. I can't tell who's in the picture."

"That is Dawn's fall off the deck," Brass said.

"This is Dawn?" Dyme squinted at the black and whites. His mouth did that munching motion Brass recognized from the interviews.

"One of the neighbors took these."

Dyme thought a minute. "Oh, Little Snoop from across the pond. But I don't get it. Why are these important?"

"I'm asking for your impression."

"I would think her arms would be flailing out to catch herself, but it sort of looks like she is floating down or something. I remember there wasn't even a splash."

"What do you know about your wife?"

"I know that she got me out of prison. If she and Connie hadn't kept on, I'd still be there. If I'd been in Texas, I'd already be executed. Dawn was a hotshot landscape architect in New York before she got interested in my case. She gave up her career for me. We fell in love. She believes—believed—in me. What else is there to know?"

"Have you met her family, her parents, any siblings? Where did she grow up? Where did she go to high school? Who are her friends? Can she swim?"

"Well, no. I don't know those things. She's told me all about her family. Right after my release, we went to New York and then New Zealand. I mean we've been all over. I haven't had a chance to meet her folks, but I will."

"Don't you think that's a little strange?"

"No. She talks to them. To her dad a lot. I hadn't thought about it, really."

"Did you know that Dawn's father committed suicide and her mother died in a car accident?"

Dyme leaned back, away from Brass. "You're not resonating with me, man. Spinning off into a hundred directions. Asking about Dawn. I'm not saying another word to you without my lawyer and he should be here by now."

"Suit yourself." Brass got up to leave. "I personally do not give a shit about you, but I have a job that requires I work from the facts. If the facts show you didn't push her, that's the way it rolls. You are, and always have been, your own worst enemy."

As Brass's hand touched the door, Dyme spoke. "Wait. I want to hear what you know about Dawn."

Brass reached into another of the files he carried and handed Dyme a death certificate for Robert Martin. "Dawn found her father hanging from a light fixture when she was twelve."

"Martin? Who? Back up, man."

"Dawn Daniels is not the name of the woman you married. The name on her birth certificate is Lauren Martin. It has never been legally changed to Dawn Daniels."

"This can't be right. Nora Ritt wrote all about her. *The New York Times* wrote about us. We've talked with several other reporters. We've been on the *Piers Morgan* show, *The View,* all over the networks. Everyone knows about me and her. If she isn't really Dawn Daniels, someone would have found out before now."

"Why would they investigate beyond what Dawn told them? She doesn't draw attention to herself. Flies under the radar most of the time. 'The Architect and the Inmate,' the Ritt article you mentioned, Ritt painted your relationship with Dawn as a fairy tale. If Dawn were to turn out to be of white trash stock, do you think anyone else would find it romantic she married you?

"Dawn, I will call her that for now, has never lived in New York City although she has a mailing address at a postal shop in Midtown. She did live in Florida, Illinois, and Louisiana. Dawn Daniels has in her name a bank account, a social security card, a job history, and no police record, all of which allowed her to pass a background check so she could visit you."

"This is surreal."

How many times had Dyme used "surreal" since he'd been out of prison? Brass wondered. In the interviews Brass had watched, it seemed to be Dyme's favorite word.

"So what if she changed her name from Lauren to Dawn? Big deal. It isn't a crime."

"Do you know the amount of money Daniels collected from your supporters before hooking up with Connie Horton?"

The change in direction confused Dyme. "Uh. What? I don't know anything about donations. Dawn does all that."

"What about the AFJ? You know what that is, don't you? The non-profit that Connie and Dawn formed. It solicits donations for your cause, you and Jamie Ball. Do you know the amount raised over the past several years?"

"I just know it's been barely enough to pay for DNA tests, all the legal stuff; the lawyers are paid for by this rock star and there's a PR guy in New York who takes care of our personal publicity and an event planner for the fund-raising events, and things like that. It's really expensive. Dawn says the donations barely pay the bills. I do know that."

"Dyme *all* your 'legal stuff' is paid for by your celebrity buddies. Not donations. The private jets, the fancy hotels, the trips, all paid by them too. Donations cover catering and banquet rooms, which Trey's handles exclusively and for which AFJ pays twice what any other customer does. A chunk of AFJ money goes to an event planning agency which, if I look deeper, I will probably find is owned by Daniels."

"Wait." Dyme held up his hands, palms toward Brass, telling him to stop. "You telling me Dawn is a fraud?"

Brass handed him a copy of the print-match showing Lauren Martin and Dawn Daniels were the same person. A mug shot stared up at him. Dyme studied it. There was a resemblance between Lauren Martin and Dawn; it was in the teeth.

Brass let it sink in.

"None of this makes any sense. What did she do?" Dyme kept his eyes on the mug shot.

"Nothing too serious but enough to have a file. She was living in Florida." He didn't tell Dyme the rest.

"Dawn lived in Florida? I don't think so, she never said. I do know she was born in West Virginia. She told me that."

"That much is true."

Brass had spent much of the previous night researching Lauren Martin, aka Dawn Daniels. She'd learned the art of the con from her mother and augmented and refined what she'd learned with her lover in Fort Lauderdale, where she'd lived for a while. Brass had found that tidbit in one of her journals, a series of tomes which seemed to cover her entire lifetime. He was having it fact-checked. There was something a little too pat about the entries.

Brass continued, "You were a find for Dawn. Sabbath Dyme, a celebrity convict who needed a crusader. If you'd never got out of prison it wouldn't have mattered to her as long as donations kept rolling in."

"Whatever Dawn did, she did it for me."

Brass turned toward the door. He needed fresh air. It opened before he got a chance to touch the handle and he almost ran head-on into Sabbath Dyme's attorney and Connie Horton.

Connie rushed past Brass and threw her arms around Dyme. "My god. What have they done to you! Don't worry. I'm going to take you home with me. I will take care of you."

Brass rolled his eyes. Now Dyme was Connie Horton's prisoner.

Chapter 16

Lauren Martin aka Dawn Daniels - May 19, 2013 — 1:00 p.m.

After parting with MB at the Flight Deck, Dawn rented a car at the Enterprise counter. Her first stop was Walmart for a throw-away cell and then the Little Rock Athletic Club. She called Ron Cole. He was leaving the shooting range and said he would meet her at his house. Dawn asked if Lisa was home. She was glad to hear Lisa and Maria Blue had gone to the arts and crafts festival at River Park. Dawn hoped Little Snoop went with them. At the club she showered, changed into yoga pants, an Athleta top, and a pair of Teva sandals. She left the club and walked down Sam Peck Road with a yoga bag on her back with the mat sticking out the top, looking like any other mother walking home after a workout session at the club.

Most days since she had become Dawn Daniels had been a chal-lenge. The hair, the common clothes, the determined posture and at-titude, the necessity to be what it took to live and work with Connie. On top of that there was the whole circus of Sabbath Dyme and the crusade, the bloggers, lawyers, reporters. She'd been stretched to the limit. Now, it was over, soon Dawn Daniels would cease to exist. Only one more detail left. Dawn pondered these things as she walked down Delphi Lane for the last time. The wacky pond families were soon to be a thing of her past. Movin' on. Dawn liked it when things ended.

Unlike most people who feared change, Dawn embraced it. Hers was a restless spirit and it had been tied too long.

Ron Cole stood at the entrance to his landscaped drive. A strange man, she thought, a wounded warrior. A man who had to invent a war every day to keep himself sane. He should have stayed in the military, she thought. Domesticity didn't suit him. Of all the people on the pond, she found him the most interesting. He had helped and not betrayed her, not said a word to Brass. He had done it for himself, not for her. Cole was a man out of time and place. To his credit, he knew it.

Ron came to her, put his muscular arm around her shoulders. He'd never touched her so completely before. He led her to the garage where he had stored the boxes she left with him.

"Dawn. Or, maybe I should call you Lauren."

With those few words she knew he had known all along. She pulled away—or tried to.

"Don't waste your energy. I'm not one of those pussy men like Dyme or Billy or Blue."

Then she saw his smile. It was genuine. She relaxed as he said, "People like us, Dawn, we don't fit, but we pretend and are fairly good at it. Let's not pretend with more words between us. They just get in the way."

Dawn thought Cole sounded downright poetic.

He took the three boxes from the shelf and put them in her newly rented car. The Subaru she had shared with Sabbath was still in Ron's drive, loaded with the things he and Connie had put in it that morning. Dawn called the leasing agency and asked them to pick it up. Dyme could find his own ride. Ron removed the sacks and boxes that held her things and put them in the trunk of her new rental.

"Thanks, Ron. I'm wondering why you've helped me without even asking me a thing, knowing what you know. Why?"

"I've watched you for over two years and you've shown me what I need to know about you. I don't need the words. You are an artist. It takes artistry to pull off what you have. You are a hunter like me. We track, we stalk, and we capture."

Dawn touched Ron on the shoulder. "You. You were the hunter who put him in the shed. I should have guessed. Thank you for that." To her surprise Dawn felt a stirring of emotion at this goodbye. She kissed him on the cheek, got into the car, and drove west to the Hampton Inn.

Chenal Valley Parkway was a busy intersection. The latest generic shopping centers and restaurants were out there. It was the type of anonymous busy interstate exit where tired drivers stopped and traveling medical salespeople stayed when selling their wares to Baptist, St. Vincent, Children's, UAMC, and the surgeons and physicians who used those hospitals. Little Rock was a regional medical center. Men and women who traveled for their jobs liked to stay in the same place week after week when on the road. They holed up at the Hampton, Holiday, or whatever. They established homes away from home in these residence type inns. They grew to know the staff who greeted them by name: the chef, the bartender, and developed friendships with the other regular men and women who were earning honor points with their brand loyalty.

"Hello, Ms. Martin," the clerk said when she checked in. "Great to see you back." She handed Dawn the room card. "Sorry we didn't have 119 but 118 was available." The clerk liked this woman, her clothes were trendy and expensive, her hair always perfect, and she was a good tipper.

"Thank you, Wendy. Good to see you again. I am so ready for a shower and one of Herb's famous martinis. Do you have any messages for me?"

Wendy checked. "No. Were you expecting one?"

Dawn laid a twenty on the counter. "Let me know if something comes in. Thanks, Wendy."

When Dawn moved in with Connie, she had also established an identity at the Hampton as one of the traveling men and women working as a pharmaceutical rep. She made friends with the chef, who quickly learned her favorites. She sat at the same table in the bar, ordered the same drink, a Grey Goose martini. It was easy enough to create an illusion with few facts when you were predictable, listened more than talked, and tipped well.

The Hampton gave her privacy from Connie, something she needed since seeing Gene Walters from time to time was a priority for her. He was the one thing from her past she was not going to give up.

Dawn pulled around the back of the Hampton where the ground floor rooms opened up to the parking lot and backed in the space for 118. Using her new cell, she called Gene.

"Where are you?" she said.

"I just checked in about an hour ago. I see you. I'm in room 119. Open your trunk, take out a few things and put them in your room."

Before she knew it, he was at her side. He slid the long box out of the back of her car and put it into his black Tahoe parked next to her.

If someone was watching, she would look like one of the many sales reps with their samples and freebies, a harried professional grabbing her carry-on out of the car and transferring a box to a colleague's larger vehicle. Gene handed her an envelope that contained a debit card, cash, a driver's license, social security card, passport. Her new identity as Charlotte Claire Hill, if or when she needed it. But for now she was Lauren Martin.

Lauren locked the car, walked to her room. She stripped the spread off the bed and folded it, something she did in every hotel room, turned down the sheets, and went into the bathroom where she took a long hot shower. She laid down on the bed with her arms stretched out straight from her sides and told herself to rest. She was running on fumes and wanted to sleep, but her mind kept thinking about Gene.

Gene Walters had a facile mind and a strong body for a fifty-six-year-old. Fencing and running kept him in shape now. Years earlier free diving had been his passion. Diving to over one hundred meters without assistance except for fins engaged the mental, the emotional, and the physical aspects of a diver to the extreme. Gene held the world record for unassisted free diving at one time. Once his record was broken, he moved on to his other love, art. Walters owned two galleries, one in Miami and the other in Lahaina, Maui. He sold and collected mainly marine art, and was proud of his large collection of contemporary sculpture. He knew and appreciated the history of each piece. Gene was the kind of collector who honored a piece of art as a life force, a being with its own history and destiny.

Lauren first met Gene on a dive boat when she was eighteen and again when she worked for art appraiser Helen Golden as her personal assistant. They had travelled down to Miami to look at a private collection and stopped by his gallery. Lauren saw an old grainy black and white photo of the gallery owner taken thirty years earlier on the day he broke the free diving record in the Bahamas. She recognized the picture. The Scuba Shack's owner had the same photograph hung in the shop when she worked there.

When Helen introduced her to Gene Walters, Lauren didn't mention she'd made the connection. Later in the day, when Helen was taking her afternoon rest, Lauren went back to the gallery. His office door wasn't closed. She stood in the opening until he looked up.

"I met you in the eighties at the Scuba Shack. You were friends with the owner. I worked on the dive boat and in the shop. I was in the water one day when you made a free dive to two hundred feet and scared our clients. They thought you were committing suicide."

He came around his desk and greeted her. Lauren was impressed. Not an ounce of fat on him. As she remembered, his smile was one of a man genetically predisposed to being happy, and his posture still erect, almost military. He wore shorts, sandals, and a tan Tommy Bahama shirt with embossed palm trees running down one side of the front.

"Lauren Martin. I thought there was something familiar about you. It was two hundred twenty-five feet, by the way. I remember you that day. The anchor was down at around one twenty, and it was caught on something. Gary put on a tank and was going down to get it free. You grabbed a pair of fins and jumped over the side before he could get in the water. I was impressed you could free dive to that depth and dislodge an embedded anchor. You were just a kid. Impressive."

"You thought I was a show-off. I made that dive because I was afraid the boat captain would get the bends. His meter was close to red. We needed the anchor. So I took care of it."

"I didn't know bends were a concern. As I remember, I liked your spunk."

That was the start of a friendship that developed around art and turned into a relationship, or as much of one as a married man could have with a woman who lived hundreds of miles away. It was Gene who educated Lauren on Calder mobiles and sculpture and other contemporary sculpture in depth. Calder, the spirited artist who viewed his metal mobiles as whimsy. It was Gene who helped her appreciate the fact that art, especially great art, or expensive art, has a life of its own as it travels from owner to owner, exhibition to exhibition. Art can break a person financially and tear apart a family.

Not all of those who love art can afford what they like. Gene had contacts with artists who copied expensive works. For certain buyers who wanted but could not afford the originals, Gene made this option available. The reproductions were not cheap but they were affordable.

Gene was the only person Lauren trusted completely. He knew about the Worthy Causes, and he didn't judge. When she told him about her Sabbath Dyme project, and her new identity, he didn't judge. When she married Dyme and moved in with Connie, he came to her because she was not always free to meet him. When she told him Connie wanted a Calder, Gene's gallery brokered the sale. When Lauren told Gene about Connie and Dyme, he asked her what she was going to do. Lauren revealed her plan and he helped her implement it. Gene knew everyone in her life but no one knew about Gene.

Lauren was anxious for Gene to return and when he did, they made love in bed at the Hampton Inn, soaking up each other, and then they talked. As usual with Gene most conversations started with a question. In that way he reminded her of MB and Little Snoop, Anna Blue.

"What is going on here in Little Rock? I thought we had a couple of more weeks. The last time we talked, you were going to change the mobiles out and then confront Dyme about his affair and leave. What happened?"

"When Connie dropped the infidelity bomb, I didn't plan to react to it until I got the Calder reproduction from you, just like we talked about on the phone yesterday. But then a lot of things out of my control happened, and I had to adjust. I told Beau Connie told me that Dyme was cheating and he said he thought Connie was cheating with Dyme. I didn't figure he was that perceptive. Then he went into this long history of his life with Connie. The more he remembered the more he worked himself up into such a high degree of anger that he went to her house and destroyed her art collection. I don't have proof it was him, but in my gut I know he did it.

"He tore up the house but he didn't touch the Calder, so I took it down and boxed it up. Then I went to Ron Cole, the ex-military guy who lives by Connie, and asked him to check the house out for me. He did and then told me to call the police. I didn't want to do that, so I told him I would tell Connie, she would want to do that herself. I wanted to delay the police coming to the house because I worried they would start looking for the Calder.

"While Ron was going through the house checking for intruders, I told him I was leaving Sabbath because he was cheating on me. I didn't have the car so I asked him if he would keep a few boxes for me. I said I didn't know how Sabbath would respond when I left, and I didn't want to leave my things behind. I took him three boxes and he put them on a shelf in his garage.

"When I boxed the Calder, I also boxed Grandmother's woodblocks and left that box in the shed. MB was on her way to pick me up in her plane. We were going to meet after my talk with Sabbath and leave together for New Orleans. Then, I asked her to stop by and get a box for me and ship it; I wanted to create a diversion. Connie had saved the original Calder boxes, a box within a box. I assumed she would take the cops to the shed and they would find the boxes gone. That would mean someone took the Calder who knew about the boxes. The police would start looking for the mobile and they would probably check UPS and FedEx. That's why I asked MB to ship a box that could contain the Calder.

"When Sabbath got home, I told him Connie said that he was cheating. He denied it a few times and finally admitted he was having sex with Connie. Can you believe it? When I first suspected, I put those spy cameras around. Got to give it to Connie, she didn't waste any time getting him to trust and then fuck her. Poor thing. Dyme not Connie. Anyway. He told me he was having sex with her so he could practice on her before he had sex with me. I saw a wonderful opportunity to create another diversion.

"I stepped into the role of a woman crazy with jealousy. He threw my computer case out the door. I ripped him deep across the face with my fingernails. He grabbed me and we fought. He made these bruises on my wrists. I got on a bench next to the deck rail and when he stepped toward me, I let myself go backward, over the rail into the water. My favorite back dive. I swam underwater until I got to the end of the pond near the highway. I ran out, cars screeched and stopped, an ambulance came, and I told the ER doc I had been assaulted by Sabbath Dyme.

"I knew when Connie reported the theft, the police would look for the Calder, and it was in Ron Cole's garage. So I made a big stink about the assault, accused Sabbath of trying to kill me, hoping they would focus on that instead of the mobile. I even convinced MB I was a woman scorned, hot for revenge. This morning, I went to Cole's place and picked up my boxes and now I am here with you."

Gene did not speak until Lauren finished her story. "You're the most complex person I've ever known and this tale raises the level considerably. And you're fearless. That's what made me remember you across all those years. Oh, did you get rid of the cameras?"

"I took those out a few weeks ago, after I found out all I needed to know. Glad I did. I'm not sure I would have remembered them in all the excitement or had time to get rid of them."

"When did the police talk to you?"

"Oh, yes, that. A detective named Brass came to my hospital room. He'd had my computer overnight and brought it with him. He set it on the bed. That little bit of non-verbal told me a lot. He intended it to. He knows my real name isn't Dawn Daniels, I am sure. He has photos of my 'fall' from the deck. That kid across the pond I've told you about took them while she was spying on me as usual.

"I think Brass suspects me of taking the Calder. I saw the detective take the glass I'd been drinking from at the hospital so I am sure he ran my prints. He probably already checked the shed and found the mobile boxes were gone. He will have to locate the postal shop that mailed it, and he will because I had MB ship it from the most obvious location, very close to Delphi. I believe he will follow that trail. I hope so.

"MB got me out of the hospital. I told her I was staying in Little Rock and not going back with her. She didn't like that. I called Missy and asked if I could stay with her awhile and then I let the police know where I could be found."

"Where do we go from here? Are we still on the same path or is there a change?" Gene didn't move from her side. He kept his left hand on her belly while he propped up his head with the right one.

"Here's what I'm thinking. First, I need to get over to Missy's soon. I'm going to keep on making a public stink about the assault to keep the cops' minds on it. Also, I am going to see a therapist. Have that on record, just in case, about the trauma I've suffered. Depending on when you let me know the Calder is safe and the repro is ready, I will have a lawyer write up an affidavit stating that I have been seeing a therapist and was suffering from a common condition among trauma victims called misattribution of memory. I'll withdraw my accusation of Dyme and apologize for accusing the police of going easy on him."

Gene asked, "What about the replica? Why even bother giving Connie that? I have several clients who would be interested in it. Calder is hot right now. I just sold a reproduction for six figures. Sure you want to turn that down?"

"Yes. I want to have the piece anonymously shipped to Connie. She is so stupid she will think it is the one she bought. If by some stretch, she suspects it is not the original, she would never tell anyone. She will hang it back up and give it a welcome home party, with a big splash about it in the paper. That would be the Connie I know."

"What about MB? How much of this has she been told?

"Nothing. She doesn't know I've been onto Dyme and Connie all along. I've left her in the dark about the Calder too. She seems upset I am accusing Dyme of assault but I can't figure out why she cares, maybe it's some lawyer thing. She says it isn't necessary to cause him trouble, but she doesn't know that it is a diversion. She did ask me if I took the Calder. I said no, and she wanted to know what was in the box. I told her the woodblocks. You are still the only human on earth who knows all my secrets."

Gene left Little Rock that evening and flew to the DFW airport where the next day he would take a flight to Hawaii. He spent several months a year there, working at his gallery in Maui. For Lauren, it felt good to be herself again, even it was only for a little more than an hour. Then she drove to the mall and found a public restroom. She went in Lauren and came out Dawn. She put on her Dawn clothes and her Dawn attitudes and drove out to Dawn's place at Missy's.

She hoped that within a week or two she could bury Dawn Daniels for good. She would like to be Lauren Martin again but if she had to assume her new name of Charlotte Claire Hill, she would.

May 22, 2013

WHERE IS DAWN DANIELS?

Daniels sneaked out of St. Vincent Infirmary the day after accusing Sabbath Dyme of trying to kill her. No one has seen her since.

Daniels is hiding, but she is aggressively using all social media to loudly claim that Dyme is dangerous and the LRPD is doing nothing to protect her and the public.

Sabbath Dyme is holed up at Connie Horton's house on Delphi Pond. Cars are lined up on both sides of the highway out there. I'm waiting for the vendors to show up with P.V. Two T-shirts and hot dogs for sale.

LRPD hasn't charged Dyme because there is no proof he pushed his wife off a deck and tried to kill her. It is a "she said he said." Or rather a "she tweeted and he did not respond."

Rumor Review

The LRPD has photos—Dawn Daniels was not pushed. She jumped. She dove.

Word is Daniels caught Dyme in a tryst and she is looking for revenge.

A two million dollar piece of art went missing from the Horton house the night Daniels claimed Dyme attacked her. That adds another dimension to this family drama. Two events make a co-incidence but three a conspiracy.

GO BOLD! Quit hiding behind your blog, Twitter, and YouTube videos, Dawn Daniels.
Give a live news conference on the steps of the LRPD headquarters.

Chapter 17

Morel Baptiste Bienville - New Orleans - 1998

MB Bienville, graduate of Tulane Law, sat at her desk studying for the bar exam when the brass knocker on her front door banged. She wasn't startled. Joe had heard the soft steps coming up the stairs and already alerted her. She opened it on the third knock, Joe taking his place at her side.

"Hello. I'm Lauren Martin," the well-dressed young woman said. "Jan at the Alligator's Purse mentioned that you had a vacancy. Did she phone you that I was coming?"

"Jan Aldrich sent you over here? That doesn't sound like her," MB said in a flat tone.

"No. I came on my own. I thought she would call to let you know I am interested. I am anxious to find a place."

MB leaned against the door frame while Joe blocked the entrance to the house. Her oversized, tie-dyed T-shirt barely came below her boxer shorts. Her long hair was held with a band in a ponytail at the side of her left ear. The wavy hair hung over her shoulder and flowed down her chest to six inches above her slim waist.

The woman in front of her was dressed like she belonged in the Junior League. Her strawberry blond hair was medium length and tucked behind her ears, showing off a beautiful pair of emerald studs set in yellow gold. She wore a smart summer suit with high heels and carried an expensive Coach bag. On her left wrist, her gold Rolex hung loose like a bracelet. Her nails were manicured and the polish a blush pink.

"When I told Jan I was looking for a place, she gave me your number." Lauren Martin handed MB a business card from the Alligator's Purse.

MB turned it over and saw her name and number.

Jan Aldrich, a transplant to New Orleans, was in her early fifties and owned the high end clothing store. She had purchased it from the original owner ten years earlier. MB didn't shop there, not her style. From the looks of Lauren Martin that was probably where she did a lot of shopping or at least wanted people to think she did.

"Are you a customer or a friend of Jan's?"

"A customer and an acquaintance. I go in the shop frequently. I love her style." Lauren hesitated before saying more. "I've been looking for an apartment in this district. This house is beautiful. The landscaping, fabulous. The neighborhood is perfect for me with the shops and restaurants nearby, and it is close to school."

MB lived in an old New Orleans mansion owned by her uncle Tad in the Carrollton District. She stayed there free in return for acting as superintendent to the four units at the back of the house. The big white structure was built a hundred years earlier in rectangular sections to imitate the look of an Italian villa. A deep porch scattered with sets of white wicker furniture wrapped around the front and sides. Decorative iron railings encased the large, shady corner lot. The drive into the property came off a side street and it required a code to get past the entrance gate.

The back of the house had been converted into four units of approximately nine hundred square feet each. Two on the top and two below. There was a common arched entrance to the apartments. The wide patio of old brick ran the length of the back of the house, and four sets of French doors from the two ground floor apartments opened onto it. Across the second story there was a balcony with four more matching doors. Red, pink, and white trailing geraniums spilled over the iron railing. Ferns in giant copper pots sat at each side of the apartments' entrances. Across the cobblestone courtyard from the apartments was an old stable that was renovated to house six cars. A large apartment had been installed above it.

Morel Baptiste Bienville was a native of New Orleans and could trace her bloodline to before the Louisiana Purchase. Children of the French and Spanish settlers born in the New World were known as Creole, and they were as much a part of southern Louisiana as the river and beignets. Morel could not imagine living any place but New Orleans or with anyone but Joe. She had no plans on reproducing to help keep the Bienville line going. Her mother had been the only girl in a family of seven boys, so there would be plenty of Bienvilles in New Orleans for a long time, even without her help.

What gave MB more comfort than any human was her dog, a Rhodesian ridgeback that she called Joe. He could have been a show dog, except there was a little something off in the ridge running along his spine and he didn't meet the breed standard. Uncle Tad had him trained as a guard dog and gave Joe to his niece on her sixteenth birthday. MB loved his dignified athletic body and expressive eyes. His was an ancient breed out of South Africa used by lion hunters to track, corner, and hold lions. Although Joe was calm with her, he was wary of strangers, another characteristic of the breed.

Joe made a little move forward. He sensed discomfort in the woman at the door. MB laid her hand on his big neck.

"Lauren. It is Lauren, right? I don't like people walking up to my door. See that gate? It doesn't have a lock on it, but it is closed. That is called implied privacy."

"Oh. I see. So it's not possible for me to see the place today?"

"I didn't say that."

MB checked her Rolex submariner, a Rolex of a different stripe than the one Lauren wore. The stainless steel watch on MB's wrist was produced between 1962 and 1982, and water resistant to six hundred sixty feet. She'd bought it secondhand. A man's watch, MB liked the heft of it against her left wrist.

"I've got some time, Lauren. Have a seat." MB indicated the wicker rocker with the floral cushion and she went back inside to call Jan Aldrich.

Lauren had taken the seat as though her feet were a little tired. MB knew her visitor had not received the greeting she'd hoped for. Jan would have told her MB was friendly, when she wasn't. Certainly, Lauren had not found her friendly.

MB, making up for her lack of manners, came back with two glasses of mint tea and handed one to Lauren. "I manage the rentals. I normally don't show the place unless the person is pre-qualified. That saves me time. You'd be surprised at the number of folks who are just curious about the property. It is magnificent. I see tons of tourists standing out front with their cameras."

"So you want me to fill out an application before you show me the place?"

"After we talk a bit, maybe I'll show you around."

"Reasonable. What do you want to know?" Lauren sipped her tea and gently rocked in the chair. It was a perfect size for her; she could get her feet flat on the ground. At five foot five, and with most of her length from the waist up, some chairs were too deep for her.

"What type of work do you do, Lauren?"

"I'm a pre-med student at the university and I work part-time."

"You work part-time and you are a college student. The rent here is not cheap. Not student housing by any stretch. When I saw you at the door, I figured you—I don't know maybe worked at a bank or real estate or something."

Lauren smiled. "I see. You are worried you are wasting your time because you think I can't pay the rent. Is that it?"

"I don't want to be rude, but—"

"I assure you I can pay the rent. I have a trust fund administered by my mother and my part-time job is actually volunteer work for an organization that collects donations for disaster victims around the country."

"The neighbors around here won't like you going up to their doors asking for donations."

Lauren gave her another smile. "I don't usually walk up to the doors of strangers like I did with you. You've got an apartment and I need one, so why not give it a try? I'm not shy. Still, I meet with potential donors by appointment only, and obviously I have to dress appropriately. Here's my business card." Lauren reached her hand out toward MB and Joe immediately planted himself between them. Lauren gasped and jerked her hand back.

"It's okay, Joe. Don't worry. He isn't going to hurt you. He is extremely well trained and your tone of voice and that quick movement of your hand got his attention. He did what he was trained to do, protect me." Joe hadn't been comfortable since Lauren came to the door.

"I see. I'm not used to being around big animals—or animals at all. I know you are busy, and I would like to see the apartment."

Lauren followed MB into the spacious entry of the main house. In the center hung a chandelier heavy with teardrop crystals, deep crown moldings were painted cream in contrast to the mango colored walls. The cherry floor was deep in color, the planks wide and waxed to a high shine. They turned right into the front room that was a mix of Spanish and French furniture, with Haitian artwork hanging on the walls. A French bergère chair reupholstered in bright turquoise linen sat next to an elegant antique French chest. A beveled glass cabinet held an assortment of waxed skulls, Virgin Mary and Christ Child statues, masks, colored glass, starfish skeletons, cowrie shells, and various other small objects.

"This is a lovely room. Eclectic," Lauren said as she took in the mixture of colors and furniture styles. "Does your family own the house? Do they live here too?"

"As I said, I manage the place. Here is an application. After I show you around, if you are still interested, fill it out and leave it with me."

Lauren and MB walked down a long, wide hall. Oil paintings depicting the history of New Orleans were set at intervals that reminded Lauren of an art gallery. MB punched a code into a locking mechanism and a door opened to the courtyard. They walked through an arch and stepped outside and took the brick walkway to the common entrance for the apartments.

"Mrs. Dickey lives on the right. She's a widow and does volunteer work too, mostly as a docent. Her daughter lives in the apartment across the hall. She's an archivist at Tulane. Upstairs on the left is Bob Sherman, he's an artist. You've probably seen his gallery on the square." They walked up the flight to the generous landing, with a door on the left and the right.

Lauren walked around the furnished apartment. The bedroom was larger than she expected with a queen size bed, a walk-in closet, and a desk. The bath was completely tiled in terra cotta with a claw foot tub, a shower, and a bidet. French doors opened off the living room and bedroom onto a balcony. She sat on the sofa, imagined herself in this space.

"Do we have a deal?"

"Not until I check your references," MB replied.

"I thought you were kidding about that." Sounding all business she said, "If you have a reservation as to my ability to pay the rent, I can make a quick trip to the bank and give you a cash deposit today."

"I always check. The owner wants it that way."

"I see. Do you have someone else interested?"

"I have a process, and I follow it. Right now, I need to get back to my books. Sit here if you like, fill out the application and leave it on the table by the front door. I'll call you in a couple of days or so."

MB left the apartment. She had to nearly drag Joe out. She sensed something was off about Lauren Martin and so did Joe. The two of them were incurably nosey when they sensed deception.

MB checked out Lauren's organization and learned the address was that of a postal shop in Midtown Manhattan. The telephone was answered by a service. She called the apartment complex where Lauren lived and learned that she always paid her rent on time, never had visitors, and was quiet, clean. The building was closer to the university than MB's place and in a less trendy neighborhood. She called the three personal references.

MB's instincts told her not all the details on Lauren matched up. As a competitive poker player, MB relied on her people reading skills. She felt something was off and for her there was only one way to get it off her mind: find the answers. She wasn't interested in Lauren as a renter. Those were easy to come by, the place was so desirable. She found the whole circumstance weird, like a setup. She didn't know why she felt that way. Maybe it was the way Lauren had appeared at her door and the scent Joe got off of her. MB had made up a story in her mind about what Lauren was about and she felt compelled to check it out.

It was an old game, this hearing a little bit of a conversation and inventing a story around it. A game she and her closest cousin, Augustus, had played since they were children. They were people watchers, eavesdroppers, storytellers. Growing up over a poker club in the French Quarter, hearing a snatch of a story here and there stoked those qualities in MB. She called Augustus after Lauren left and he came over. It wasn't a long journey to get to her front door, he lived in the apartment over the converted stable. Uncle Tad was Augustus's father, so Augustus had been given first choice of the apartments.

After an hour of speculation about Lauren they had developed a couple of scenarios of who this stranger was and why she had appeared at their door. They called another cousin, Tommy Joe, for whom MB had named her dog. He had worked for the FBI before going out on his own as a private investigator. He could check Lauren's social security number and the fingerprints she'd left on the tea glass, which Augustus had already put in an evidence bag and tagged. The whole adventure of figuring out Lauren's story made them happy. A mystery to solve was something they both enjoyed.

The following week, MB contacted Lauren and asked her to stop by if she was still interested in the apartment. Lauren arrived dressed in faded jeans, wearing a tank top, carrying a backpack, she looked younger than before and like any other college student. MB almost didn't recognize her when she and Joe opened the door.

"I take it that I passed the background check." Lauren smiled.

"Thought we might celebrate with drink out here on the porch and go over the rules of what we call 'the compound' before you sign the lease. Have a seat. How about a gin martini?"

"That sounds great. Thanks."

MB left the porch. Joe sat down across from Lauren and it made her nervous. She didn't like big dogs—or dogs at all. The little ones she especially couldn't stand. Lauren didn't have pets but she was more of a cat person. They were self-reliant and not into pleasing people.

MB brought out the makings of a martini, gin, vermouth, the shaker, glasses, olives, and made the drinks at the glass table in front of the wicker love seat.

"How's your mom? I believe you said she was living in North Carolina?"

"She is just great."

Tommy Joe learned Laura Martin, Lauren's mother, had died in a car accident when Lauren was eighteen, and her father had hung himself when Lauren was twelve. She was born in West Virginia, an only child.

"I am an only child too. My mom and I are real close. So you know what that means: you will probably meet her. She is gorgeous. Runs a poker club, believe it or not."

"I don't recall telling you I was an only child." Lauren studied MB. "Well, I know what you mean about the special bond. Believe me. I sure do."

"What brought you down to Louisiana for college? Why not go to Duke? It's a great school and has a beautiful campus."

"I felt like I needed some space from my mother while staying fairly close. New Orleans has so much mystery, it's romantic, and I like that."

"When do you graduate? You realize the lease is for a year."

"No problem. Next spring. If I'm lucky enough to get in Tulane, I'd stay on while I'm in med school."

Lauren had fifteen hours of college credit at various colleges and those classes were in art history subjects and business, according the Tommy Joe's report. Lauren Martin had a record in Florida. A few DUI's, one resulting in an overnight stay and a disorderly conduct from when she was twenty-one. She'd worked in a scuba shop, had a fairly long relationship with a married boat captain and that seemed to settle her down. She moved to Fort Lauderdale after that and lived with a man who owned a string of consignment shops in Florida, plus a couple of bars and restaurants.

They determined Lauren was a con artist setting up a grift in the New Orleans area. She'd registered the organization as a nonprofit charity with the proper state offices. If someone looked into it and didn't dig too deep, it would look legitimate. She solicited donations and clothing, jewelry, portable items, and of course accepted cash, checks, and credit cards.

With the clothing and jewelry, she separated out the high end pieces and sent them to the upscale consignment shop in Lauderdale. She kept a generous percentage of the proceeds. The next tier of clothing went to a middle income consignment place, and so on down the food chain until the clothes were just fit for Goodwill and that's where she sent them. Monetary donations went into the organization's bank account and eventually found their way into Lauren's pocket.

What Lauren was very good at doing was soliciting donations one-on-one from women. In Augustus's opinion, she could have legitimate work as a fund-raiser, but he suspected she was hooked on her way of life. She'd carried out the same con in other areas where she could pose as a college student working as an intern for the organization, or a housewife, divorcee, or whatever she needed to be to attract the class of donor she was targeting. She rented apartments in or near trendy upscale neighborhoods and made herself known, a frequently seen presence shopping in the neighborhood, jogging, having a latte at the local coffee shop.

When MB and Augustus got the report, they of course argued over who was more right than the other.

"She stalked me. I knew she did. I get a check for that," MB said.

"Coincidence," Augustus countered.

They both guessed she wasn't a college student. That was a no-brainer so neither got credit. It was in going over the report that Augustus had the idea that they should rent the place to Lauren so they could observe a grifter up close.

"It will be like having an exotic bird living in our midst," Augustus said. "I bet she will only stay a year. That's been her pattern in each place she's rented, and she always pays her rent. She will probably say she got into med school in Florida or someplace."

"I agree about the move. I think she is going to come up with some other cover when she moves on. She's getting a little too old to carry on that student act."

After her lease was up, Lauren did move away from New Orleans to North Carolina, saying she'd gotten into med school there. Then to Chicago. She kept in touch with MB and visited her in New Orleans occasionally. It was during one of these visits that Lauren told her story, her talents for the grift, how she learned from her mother and her grandmother, and she told MB about her father's hanging.

MB asked why the confession and Lauren said, "I'm ready for someone to like me for who I really am. You are the only woman I've met that I think won't judge me. I want a friend."

MB did not confess she knew the story all along. She had her own secrets. She liked Lauren, her spunk, her talent, and that she led a life MB could not imagine. Both women were clever in ways that complemented each other and quickly they were more than friends. They became a team.

Chapter 18

Augustus Baptiste Bienville - New Orleans - 2000

MB's reasons for getting Dyme out of prison and now keeping him out were family reasons. Reasons she didn't share with anyone. To tell Lauren, after all this time of her not knowing, was unthinkable. It could harm MB's favorite cousin, Augustus.

Not really a cousin though, actually MB's twin brother, born four minutes later, weighing two pounds more, and raised by Uncle Tad as his son. While MB was honey blond, with dark brown eyes, and olive skin, Augustus's hair was black, eyes blue, and his complexion creamy. The feature they had in common with all Bienvilles was full lips, straight teeth, and a big smile that came easy. MB hadn't known she had a brother until a visit with a psychic alerted her to an unknown "womb mate." Another psychic alluded to the same thing. MB used psychics and tarot card readers as a way to stimulate her imagination, not plan her life. She didn't believe or disbelieve, she was as agnostic in this area as she was in the belief of god.

MB asked her mother, Alexi, if she had given birth to twins and one had died. Her mother denied the twin and didn't tell MB her secret until it had to be told. Tad, Alexi's favorite brother, was sterile. His wife had wanted to adopt but Tad had refused because the child wouldn't be a true Bienville. When Alexi learned she was pregnant with twins, she promised Tad one of the babies. One was enough for her to raise alone.

They came up with a plan to hide the truth and vowed the secret would stay between the three of them. Alexi gave Tad her boy.

Tad didn't know Alexi eventually broke her vow and his favorite niece knew his secret. No one else in the family knew for sure that Morel and Augustus were fraternal twins instead of first cousins. Augustus, with his round blue eyes, wiry black hair, small ears, and sturdy forehead, had a thickness about him that spoke of an underlying physical strength, like that of a South Pacific islander, bones the size of two-by-fours. Legs like a rugby player, powerful, but for his eyes which were soft and barely blue with darks specks sprinkled at random, he would have looked like a brute.

Augustus wasn't especially tall, six feet or so, and weighed in at about one ninety-five of pure muscle. Hands strong enough to break a brick with one strike yet soft enough to play classical piano, which he did quite well, although his preferred instrument was electric guitar. It was portable, he could wield it like a weapon, play it hard, loud, nervous.

Tad adored Augustus but one winter it became apparent his boy was suffering and no one knew why. He'd lost interest in his music, in his life. It happened suddenly, and Tad feared it might be schizophrenia. Alexi thought the reason was psychic, that he was feeling the circumstances of his birth.

The extended Bienville family was present when the shift occurred. All forty plus of them had come together at Tad's for Alexi's birthday. As usual when they gathered, they spent their time cooking, playing poker, shooting pool, eating, laughing, the things a big family does together when they enjoy each other. The party was winding down when someone turned on the television in Tad's new media room and an HBO documentary appeared on the screen. It was about two men in prison who were accused of killing three little boys in the mid 1990s in West Memphis, Arkansas.

Tad was in and out of the room not paying too much attention but Augustus, MB, and the other cousins were glued to the television. Every one of them had a different take on the subject—independent thinking was something that defined a Bienville, a trait that was encouraged. Tad could not tolerate the Sabbath Dyme character. That's how Tad thought of him, a character. The other boy was irrelevant, a follower. MB thought right away Dyme was a killer, an opportunistic one, not a planner, who had an inflated opinion of himself, and from there all the cousins had an opinion. Tad loved the family's energy and so did Alexi. They were at their most contented when everyone was together.

When the evening ended, Augustus asked Tad if he could stay in his old room. Tad didn't think too much about it, but it did strike him as a little strange. He'd not stayed over since he'd moved into his own apartment. In spite of his size, Augustus had a soft side. He looked tired to Tad and he thought his son needed the comfort of his old bedroom.

It went on for a year, this malaise, depression, this—Tad didn't know what to call it—this possession of unseen spirits. Augustus lost interest in his music, his workouts at the gym, the event planning business he and MB owned together. Usually he managed the business, and was good at the job. It gave him a venue for his music. Augustus often booked his band as backup for celebrity bands or as an intro to other performances. He had forward thinking ideas and was good at marketing. Now he was absent and MB had to hire a manager while she waited for Augustus to right himself, but he didn't.

People move to New Orleans from other states or countries and live there many years, but they are not considered locals by the citizens who were born and raised there. Those families with the Bienville history don't consider anyone a local unless their family was there before the Louisiana Purchase. It was all a matter of degree. Romantic beliefs outsiders have about New Orleans, voodoo, psychics, Creoles, and Cajuns, added a lot to the economy. Locals with the Bienville history did not go down to Bourbon Street looking for a poultice, or a tarot card reading, or a psychic encounter to cure what ailed them. Real shamans or kahunas, or whatever one chose to call a practitioner with an insight into the unknown, did not take American Express, Visa, or MasterCard. They didn't dwell in the land of tourism.

Tad did the only thing he thought would work, the thing he always did when his heart was broken. He went to his sister, Alexi. But Tad didn't know how bad his heart was broken until he said to her, "Our boy is dying and I don't know what to do." Alexi did. She collected Augustus and they went south. Where they went, Tad didn't know or ask. In the spring when they returned, Augustus was back among them.

Augustus sought out MB when he felt well enough. He needed her advice, her understanding, and the comfort he'd always gotten from her since they were children. Their relationship was not unlike that of Alexi and Tad. No woman could measure up to MB, in Augustus's estimation, so he didn't look for one. He was a loner and liked it that way. It was a comfortable way to exist and when he got old enough he realized MB was the same—alone and preferring it that way.

MB made tea. She sat down with Augustus, who started slow, looking down at his feet. "I don't know how my mind could have sealed off this memory for so long. The healer said my soul was protecting me because the memory of what happened was too strong for my psyche to handle. When the cracks in my psyche opened, and the memories started rising, my spirit sealed them off again, but there was a residue left behind and that was crippling me. Now I can tell it to someone besides the healer and in the telling I will release it and then I can do what it takes to heal myself. She says I need permission to share this memory with you."

"Anything. No need to ask." MB took both his hands in hers and could feel that his strength was returning, yet it wasn't nearly back to where it had been.

"Remember the event we did in the mid nineties, the one at Mud Island, for the president of First Tennessee? It was summer. We booked James Taylor. There was a thunderstorm the night he played. He said something to the crowd about the storm being an omen. I booked Dash Rip Rock too and my band played as warm-up. I'd been staying at Harbor Town for a week to set things up and had pulled my boat down there so I could cruise up and down the Mississippi.

"You'd just gotten your pilot's license and flew up in your new Cessna. Remember, we flew low over the woods across the river from Memphis, we saw some deer along the trails. The traffic controller got all over you."

MB said, "I remember that clearly. I could have lost my license. We had a great time. We've done a number of big events for that bank. What made this one different?"

"When the tent was folded up, so to speak, I stayed on a couple of days. One of the guys from Dash Rip gave me a peyote button. I thought that was an omen. I needed some inspiration for my music, and well, the Indians have been finding deep introspection and insight in peyote for over five thousand years. Why not me? I'd never done it before and didn't know what to expect. I chewed the button and got into the boat and started cruising the Arkansas side. I threw up over the side of the boat. Then the visions started. I don't know how, but I found a sand bar and tied the boat to a big log stuck in it and started wandering around the woods.

"For several years that was all I remembered about that day except for parts of one vision. I called it the Tower Vision because from it I got the idea of having a tower built for me to stand on when I played with the band. Only thing is, now I don't know if it was a vision or a real happening. When I saw the P.V. Two film, I remembered something, and I don't know what to do about it."

"You know you can tell me anything. I'll just listen. But when you finish is it okay if I ask questions?"

"You are the same as always. Listen and ask a ton of questions. I'll start with the tower vision."

Augustus pushed back the soft leather recliner and shut his eyes. MB settled on the floor and sipped her passion flower tea.

"I am following a path, walking through the woods. The light is making flickering shadows. I hear whispers and animals walking on pine needles and dry leaves, their eyes looking at me. I see a tower and I climb the ladder. It is made of split logs lashed to a tremendous tree trunk that rises twenty feet high. There are no branches on the tree, instead a platform is sitting on top of the big trunk.

"Lying in the middle of the platform is a guitar. I pick it up and start playing and as I play faster and faster I grow taller and taller. My head is above the other trees when I feel something, many somethings, crawling up my legs.

"They are the size of little boys and look like warriors: mean, laughing, biting my legs, crawling fast. I try to shake them off, but they keep coming. My guitar turns into a fiddle and I start playing 'Devil Went Down to Georgia.' The faster I play the faster they climb my legs. The fiddle turns into a cello and I use it like a weapon and start hitting them. They fall to the ground. I pick up three of them and toss them over the sides of the platform into a creek. I hear their bodies break and when that happens the other devil boys deflate like balloons and I am standing alone on the tall platform playing the guitar and there is a crowd down below cheering and clapping.

"I don't remember much about getting back except pulling up to Mud Island Harbor just before sundown.

"The night we saw the P.V. Two film, when I saw Sabbath Dyme, I realized that I knew him from that day. I'd not seen the other guy, but I had seen him. And this is the part that has dealt me the blow that started my life crumbling.

"I remembered that I found myself lying on my back, and I was in a deer hunting stand. Maybe it was ten feet or so off the ground. There was a creek nearby. I was hot and very thirsty, so I climbed down and walked to the creek to cool off. There, next to the bank, I saw three sleeping boys. At least I thought they were sleeping. As I looked closer I saw they were dead. They had on shorts and shoes and no shirts.

"I noticed an animal path leading to the water, but I would have to cross the creek to get to it. I wanted to run away. As I was rolling up my jeans, I heard a sound coming from that direction. I thought it was a bear. It sounded like something big. So I ran back the way I came as quietly as I could and climbed the deer stand and laid flat. I was still high and kind of paranoid I guess.

"It wasn't a bear. It was a young man or teenager. He was chubby and wore his black hair long. He was dressed completely in black and carried a black backpack. He knelt at the creek and scooped up some water to drink. Then I guess he saw the boys on the other bank because he bolted upright and stood rigid. He did absolutely nothing, just looked across the creek at them. He walked a little upstream to some rocks that made a makeshift path and crossed to where they were.

One boy was on his back. He turned him over. The other two were facedown. Then he took his pack off and laid it on the bank and removed some objects that looked like little statues or crosses and placed them in a formation of some sort. He appeared to be careful to get the placements just right. After he finished with that, he picked up each boy and laid them on the bank side by side.

"After he had them laid out, he removed their shorts, underwear, and shoes, and arranged their bodies in another formation. He was fastidious about this arrangement and he didn't seem pleased with it at first. Then he took the laces out of their shoes and tied each arm to each leg. Again it took him a while before he was satisfied. After that, he took a book out of his pack and started chanting and reading. He had a candle, a black one, and matches, and incense. It looked like some type of satanic worship to me. When he was finished with all of that, he took a pocketknife and cut his wrist and drank his own blood. He looked like he was about to walk away when another boy came along. They seemed to be friends. They hung around for a while and then left together.

"When I saw Sabbath Dyme, I recognized him as the body arranger and the blood drinker. He was as creepy in the film as he was back then. As this memory came back so did the vision of the tower. I still do not know if the tower was a vision or if it was real. I fear that I may have thrown those boys off the deer stand during my peyote trip and killed them. I just don't know. It's been eating me alive."

MB sat in silence, afraid to speak, afraid that whatever she said would be the wrong thing to say. She needed Augustus to open his eyes and look at her. She waited until he was ready to face her.

The blue eyes opened and she thought she saw the old Augustus. She wasn't sure until he spoke. "I need you to ask me every conceivable question it takes to find out what happened. I trust you. Only identical twins could be closer in spirit than we are. Maybe we were twins in a past life or maybe we will be in another life."

MB wanted to tell him the secret but knew better. Alexi had told her Augustus was her twin when he became so ill that she took him south to get him the help he needed. MB was afraid he might go back over the edge if he learned the truth, and she couldn't take that chance.

It took her a while to sort through the information. MB read every document relating to the murders. There was no evidence or speculation that the boys were thrown to their deaths, nowhere was that even floated as a possibility. That convinced her Augustus did not kill the boys. But perhaps Sabbath Dyme had killed them, left the scene to get his worshipping materials, and then Augustus found the bodies before Dyme came back to perform the ceremony. On the other side of it, he may have had those items with him when he found the three dead children, seen an opportunity to perform his perverted ritual, and done so. Coincidence. From the testimony, he was known to carry satanic type items with him in a pack, so this was possible. MB simply did not know what to think. If Augustus had had the presence of mind to report it to the sheriff when he found the boys, then Dyme and his friend may not have been convicted or even accused of the crime, or they may have.

Once MB went over the evidence with Augustus and assured him that he was not a killer, he wanted to go to the prosecutor and tell them his story, that might be enough to persuade a judge to give the boys, now men, a new trial.

"Augustus, the only people who would believe that story are Dyme groupies. You will be thought of as just another nut confessing to a famous crime. You're not responsible for what happened to Sabbath Dyme, he chose to stop and perform his vile ceremony. If you keep on with the 'what if' you are going to make yourself sick again. Tell me this, deep in your soul, do you think he did it, killed those boys? Do you?"

"I don't think he did. When he saw the bodies, he looked surprised. Then he saw an opportunity. The way he kept his eyes on them when he crossed the creek. It was very creepy. He was creepy. The sick way he undressed them, the way he took his time and looked them over, and arranged and rearranged the naked bodies. The way he tied them up. It was grotesque. Another thing. When he came along, I could have said something to him. Instead I ran. I thought I was afraid of a bear but I was really just a coward. I'd had the Tower Vision. Maybe at the time I thought I had tossed them off the tower and killed them. I don't know what I thought or if I even had a thought. Maybe I was protecting myself. I feel guilty now about them being in jail when it might be because I was weak and ran away."

"I understand. If getting them out of prison eases your mind I will do it. Be clear. I am doing it for you not for Sabbath Dyme."

Chapter 19

Lenne Vee - Anna Blue

T alk was one thing to Anna Blue. She liked to ask questions and get answers, but she loved writing even more. Especially writing her blog, LenneVeeTruthPortal. When writing it, she used the computer at the library near her school or at the postal shop at the center on Highway 10 near her house instead of her own. She had paid for her Blogspot with a pre-paid credit card. She knew she wasn't immune to discovery but the only person she truly feared finding out was her father. Anonymity gave her freedom to express the thoughts that made the grown-ups uncomfortable. Lenne had a Facebook page, a blog, Twitter, and a Gmail account. The best part, after only a little over a year, Lenne Vee had a few thousand followers. There was, apparently, a need for a mind like hers.

Lenne Vee posted the account of Dyme pushing Dawn into the pond the morning after it happened and she noticed a bump up in the number of hits on her site. Feeling emboldened that she had inside knowledge and could use it anonymously, Anna let her fingers fly and her opinions flow.

Anna looked at Sabbath Dyme as a human collage. He was like a Photoshop creation of a person who appeared to be an actual human but was constructed from several pictures cut and pasted together to look like one. In some ways Dawn Daniels was just the same. Anna hadn't made that connection until re-reading her files on the two of them after the pond incident. It was then that it occurred to her Dawn had lied because she was jealous and wanted revenge. That was a reason Lenne Vee couldn't defend or respect. Lenne believed in justice and, just as important, Lenne liked to stir things up and see how the public responded.

Several days after the incident the police still hadn't publicly mentioned the photos of the dive. Lenne Vee couldn't condone that, people deserved to know the truth, so she put the pictures on Lenne's Facebook page. It was with a little apprehension, but Anna figured they belonged to her, and she wasn't breaking the law—she didn't think.

No one seemed to know where Dawn had gone and the only words heard from her were her cryptic Twitter comments and the YouTube film of her bruised arms and call for help. Sabbath Dyme was holed up with Connie on the pond.

Anna was sitting on the bench at the edge of her property with her iPad reading other blogs when Dyme walked out of Connie's house with a suitcase. A man that looked to Anna like a bodyguard was with him. Connie came out of the house, crying. Drama. Anna watched and then moved closer to the action when she noticed Ron on his deck. She walked faster along the path at the edge of the pond, past the weeping willow Dr. Billy had added to the garden. As she got closer to Cole, he motioned for her to join him.

"It looks like Dyme is leaving Connie's house," Anna said.

"I sure as hell hope so. It's only going to get worse around here. Those Dyme lovers, perverts all of them. I've been following this damn blogger Lenne Vee. He is stirring up a shitload of trouble."

"Who?"

"Vee. God, you've got to know him. Bloggers might live like moles in their basements, but they can reach the whole world. He is probably some fat wannabe cop. Anyway, he's a troublemaker and now he is taking up for Dyme. Hell, if you ask me, the world is coming to an end when Vee takes a stand against a woman."

"I don't get what you are trying to tell me."

"Get on that damn computer of yours and go to LenneVeeTruthPortal. Vee put those pictures you gave Brass on Facebook. How in the hell did he get them? It'll probably turn out it's a Photoshop thing. For once, Dawn's out there doing the right thing, trying to put that baby killer back in jail and Vee is collecting an army against her. We've got a reality show going on down here."

Anna couldn't believe what she was hearing. Ron Cole followed her blog. He was reading her words. She wasn't even tempted to tell him she was Lenne Vee though.

"I didn't know you were into the blogosphere."

"I'm not, but I keep up with Vee. Lisa turned me on to him. He's a clever dude. I'm thinking I ought to let him know what commotion his latest antic has caused. If I had a camera right now, I could take what's in front of me and send it to him."

What was in front of Ron and Anna was Dyme, walking up the driveway with a suitcase and Connie following behind him with her arms outstretched. Anna raised her iPad.

"I'll do it." She took the picture. She was thinking about the headline she would write. The questions she would pose. The comments her readers would send.

"I'll send the picture to your Facebook."

"Lisa is the Facebook person. Send it to her." Ron thought any person who participated in Facebook was a fool and that included his wife. As long as Lisa didn't mention him, he put up with it.

"Why's he leaving?" Anna asked Ron.

"His car is at the top of the drive. Connie rented that Jeep for him. The leasing company picked up the one Dawn and he used," Ron said.

"I mean, leaving the pond. It's safe here."

"Maybe not," Cole said. "Dawn knows where he is. She could set him up. Hell, Dawn might push Connie in the water herself, hold her down, and Dyme would get the blame. Dawn is one determined woman. I wouldn't put anything past her. Every time I look at that wall she built with her bare hands, I am reminded of her grit. I wouldn't underestimate her."

Anna asked Cole, "So why are you helping Vee by sending him a scoop? You don't like Dyme. Sounds like this Vee guy will just create more sympathy for him."

Ron Cole looked at her. "You're a smart kid. Maybe I just like to stir the shit a little, see what crawls out from under the rock, however you want to put it. Better Dyme leaves our pond before he gets locked in that shed again. Next time he might not be so lucky as to get out. Plenty of snakes around now and the shed isn't snake proof."

"Do you think someone would put him in there with snakes? I hadn't thought of that. Wow. Wouldn't that be something. Who do you think did it? Put him there the first time, I mean. I used to think Beau but he is too much of a coward for that. Dyme's kind of a little guy, so maybe it was Dawn. Maybe she dived off the rail, hid, hit him with a shovel, and dragged him to the shed. I can see her doing that."

Ron Cole was almost in awe of Anna's imagination. "That's a possibility. She could have tied him up and then run out to the highway. Good thought. Makes sense to me. He better watch out. Dawn's still out there."

Dyme's lawyers were watching out for him. They got him a bodyguard and arranged for him to live in one of the loft apartments in the new Mann on Main building in downtown Little Rock. It was close to the River Market and an easy walk to the Clinton Presidential Library. Dyme lovers worried about the same things Ron described and his lawyers advised him to stay inside the loft apartment with his bodyguard.

Dyme looked out the front window of the new apartment in a building built over one hundred years earlier; for many of those years it had been occupied by the Blass Department store. The building, which was a now a combination of office space, multi-family lofts, and commercial offices, had as its main tenant the state of Arkansas. His loft, or safe house as he thought of it, ironically sat above the Arkansas Crime Information Center.

He wondered how many millions were being spent by the Moses Tucker and Doyle Rogers companies, probably not their own money, to transform Main Street. Transformation. Main Street was getting what Sabbath needed. Was he ever going to get out of one kind of prison or another? Connie smothered him and he was glad when his lawyers advised him to move away from the pond.

With Dawn he had personal space. She wasn't always touching him or rubbing his shoulders and doing acupressure on his feet. But Dawn could be a little cold when they were out of sight of the public. He found he preferred that to the cloying attention of Connie. It was the loss of privacy that disturbed him the most. "How do you feel?" "What are you thinking?" "Do you need anything?" "Can I get you something to eat?" Connie never quit being available.

Dyme's attorney said he had everything he needed there. On the wall over a solid oak credenza hung a flat screen television that looked to be about five feet wide, with speakers, subwoofers, every premium channel. The bar was fitted out with high end tequila, whiskey, gin, vodka, imported beer. The bedsheets were high thread count, the furniture trendy. The loft was just a fancy cell. He wondered how long he would be imprisoned here.

LenneVeeTruthPortal.com

SABBATH DYME FLEES
DELPHI - MAY 25, 2013

Here is a sampling of the questions coming in to LenneVeeTruthPortal:

Why did Dyme leave the sanctuary of Dephi Pond?
Did he leave the city too?
Did someone try to kill him?
Do the police even know he left Delphi?
Was he threatened by the neighbors?
Is he on the run from the cops?
Is he in protective custody?
Who kidnapped him and put him in a shed with snakes the night he "assaulted" Dawn?
Did he really try to kill Dawn?
Where are his Hollywood friends?
Have his celebrity buddies abandoned him?
Is he being framed by Dawn Daniels?
Was he cheating on Dawn with a college girl?
Why isn't he in jail since he is on parole and accused of a violent crime?
Why don't the police tell us what is going on?
What are the police hiding?
Are the police afraid of being sued by Dyme?

Why are the police taking so long to charge or not charge Dyme with assault?
Is LRPD afraid Dyme's supporters will riot in the city if he is charged?

**The questions tell me the LRPD is doing a terrible job of informing the public.
Maybe Little Rock needs a new police chief.**

Chapter 20

Wye Mountain - Brass and MB Bienville - May 23, 2013

ill Brass liked plenty of space around him and the privacy it brought him. When he took the job with the LRPD he bought a place west of town on Highway 10 in Perry County on a mountain called Wye. He drove past Delphi Pond twice a day on his way to and from the station. He never gave it a thought, but now his eyes turned toward it each time he passed.

Brass enjoyed the drive west once he got past the shopping centers that had sprung up since he'd moved out there. After he crossed Lake Maumelle and turned north on Highway 113, he stretched the limits of his black Porsche Boxster S on the curvy two lane road for five miles before turning off on a dirt road that went a half mile into the woods and ended at the edge of a high meadow surrounded halfway around by old growth pines and oaks. The rock and cedar house nested in the trees at the edge of the meadow. Ironic, he thought, a dirt road when the man who once owned the property paved roads for a living.

Brass had bought the five acres and rambling house from the estate of an asphalt contractor named Manny who grew up in North Little Rock. At sixty-four years old, Manny had sold his business to his son and planned to spend time traveling the inland waterways in his live-aboard boat, making his way to the Gulf and then the Keys. A few days after his going away party, Manny went to the doctor because of a nagging ache in his back and found he had kidney cancer and died four months later. The house with all its contents went on the market.

Wye Mountain suited Brass. The house started out many years earlier as a cabin. Over time, it had grown into a seven room house, with a game room large enough for a pool table, a bar, a fireplace the size of a small room. It reminded Brass of a saloon. Buffalo, moose, and elk heads hung along three of the walls, along with mounted trout, salmon, and other species of fish. The vaulted ceilings and skylights complemented the natural cedar walls and stone floors, giving the rooms plenty of natural light.

Manny, twice divorced and unmarried when he died, had a steady girlfriend ten years his junior. He was a cook, or maybe it would be better to call him a fan of kitchen gadgetry who enjoyed cooking in a show kitchen. Manny threw big parties judging from the number of pots, pans, skillets, Dutch ovens, fryers, griddles, dinner plates, platters, serving pieces, cutlery, carving knives, and the massive size of the stainless refrigerator which stood independent of the matching freezer. It looked like a catering business had operated out of the kitchen.

The kitchen floor was cut quarry rock in shades of gold, amber, and brown, the same rock floor carried out to a patio and traveled to the pool area where it surrounded the twenty-meter pool, making a fifteen foot wide deck around it. On the far side of the pool stood a gazebo with an outdoor kitchen, and a smoker big enough to accommodate a small goat on a spit.

Brass bought the house with all the furnishings, bed linens, towels, and accoutrements, including the animal heads and twenty pounds of deer meat packaged in various cuts in the freezer from Manny's trustee, who happened to be a friend of Brass's chief.

Quiet, remote, with a view of the lesser hills below, Brass found his paradise in what he thought of as the homeland. That's what he called Perry County, the place where his mother and father were born, and their parents too, and so were he and his sister. They moved to Colorado when he was young, and so he didn't remember much of Arkansas. But he had a feeling of coming home when he first stepped foot on the meadow of Manny's place.

When Brass heard the *thuck, thuck, thuck* of the helicopter circling his meadow, growing louder as it descended, he felt invaded and reached for the shotgun he kept near the front door. The pilot landed, soft and controlled, shut down the machine, waited for the blades to stop, and got out. Her passenger stepped out and they walked toward him. He recognized the pilot as the woman he'd seen at the hospital.

"Hello, Detective Brass. Morel Bienville. We met at the hospital outside of Dawn Daniels's room. This is my flight instructor, Paul Black. I'd like very much to visit with you a little while. I do apologize for my rude intrusion, but what I have to say is very important to the case you are working on."

MB extended her hand for a shake. She wore khaki slacks, a short sleeve white button-up shirt, black work books. Her dark blond hair was pulled back in a braid close to the nape of her neck, and aviator sunglasses covered what he remembered as big brown eyes. To Brass, she looked like a military woman the way she carried herself, not the sexy babe he encountered at the hospital.

Brass laughed. "Well, shit. I don't know what to think, or say. You've stumped me to the point where I am mute. I want to be mad that you've trespassed on my land, invaded my privacy, scared the wildlife with your flying machine, but I am intrigued."

"Good. I hoped for that." She gave him the famous Bienville smile and it was sincere. From their first meeting at the hospital, MB had had a good feeling about the detective. Gesturing to Black with her left hand she said, "If you don't mind, I think Paul would be more comfortable in one of the pool chairs instead of the helicopter."

"There is a shady patio in the back of the house. He can hang out there. As for you, come on in and I will impress you with my kitchen and you can tell me what this raid is all about."

MB removed her aviators and put them in the front left pocket of her shirt. The three of them walked to the kitchen. Paul Black, the instructor, who was dressed in attire identical to MB's, accepted a cold lemonade and Brass showed him the patio. MB walked around the kitchen waiting for him to return. Brass poured her an iced tea and motioned for her to sit at the old oak table with five legs. The table had belonged to Manny's grandmother and had spent much of its life on a farm in Cabot, Arkansas. When the old woman died, Manny took it, had it refinished, and brought it up to Wye.

MB ran her hands along the top and sides of the table. "This is a piece with history. I can feel it in the grain. It's not yours, is it? You're not the type of man who hauls his history around with him."

"Now you are spooking me." Brass liked her spunk, but he wasn't sure about her motives. "Are you psychic or did your investigation of me go that deep?"

"I was guessing. I don't know what to think about this kitchen. I didn't figure you for the gourmet type. So I'm not going to claim to be a psychic, but I'm from New Orleans and that should tell you a whole lot about me and my methods."

"I thought I heard Creole in your accent."

"Look, I don't want to waste your time. You can question me if you like, or you can let me explain, and then ask questions."

"I don't like being ordered about. You're the one who thought it important to swoop down on me from the sky, so you keep talking." Brass didn't need a recorder or a notebook, his memory for the spoken word was what a photographic memory was to the written.

"I'll start with why I am here. Dawn Daniels. I know you have found out that is not her legal name. I'm betting your tech team has gained access to her secure off-site storage and have learned a great deal about her—or think you have.

"I'm sure you are curious how I found your hideout here. My uncle is a banker in New Orleans, he has contacts all over the place. Add that to my connections as a lawyer. After the incident on the pond, I asked him to look into you. You were born in Perry County, not far from here, and moved to Colorado as a child. You played college football, you have an undergraduate degree in accounting and a master's in history, and worked as a detective for twenty years in Denver. You moved to Little Rock because of the chief here. You were college roommates. He needed an inside man and you needed a change in your life. The reason, a case you didn't solve in time resulted in another child's death. You wanted a change.

"For over ten years, you have written episodes for various television crime shows under a pseudonym and have made quite a good living off that. More than enough for you to write a check for this place. The deed is recorded in your sister's name, Barbara Brass.

"I came to ask for your help."

Brass was flummoxed. His made his face remain impassive. He stood, walked over and opened the refrigerator, and took out a cold Stella. He would have liked a Duvel but he was out. He gestured to MB with the bottle. She shook her head no.

"All of this information you have about me, and I am not saying it is correct, where did you get it?"

"Like I said. My uncle."

Brass wasn't amused any longer. He was angry. His eyes hardened along with his body. His stance went from relaxed to on guard. "What do you want?"

"Dawn is determined to put Dyme back in prison and I don't want that to happen."

"Why? Are you in on her game? You don't want it to end but now she does?"

"What makes you think that?" MB rose from the chair. She didn't like anyone standing over her.

"You came to her rescue at the hospital. You are here asking me to let Dyme go. What else am I to think?" Brass kicked the chair out from the table giving himself distance from her and sat down with the back of the chair facing her, his legs straddling the seat.

"Brass. Do you really think Dyme assaulted her?" MB stayed standing.

"It is being looked into."

"I hear you think it doesn't look like she was pushed."

"Where did you hear that?"

"Dawn or Lauren. Which name do you want to use?"

"Dawn. That seems to be the part she is playing right now and has been for a number of years. What is your connection with her?"

MB told Brass about first meeting Lauren, their history together, and something that surprised him.

MB said, "A client came to me shortly after the HBO film came out. He was in the woods the day the children were killed. He was walking a path and came across three dead boys next to the creek. He heard something and hid. He watched Dyme when he came across the bodies. Apparently, Dyme was surprised to find them. He undressed the boys, tied them up, arranged their bodies in a formation, and then he performed a ritual. After Dyme left, my client left the woods the way he came in."

"Why didn't he report it? Or, are you telling me your client killed those boys?"

MB shook her head. "No, not that. At the time, he was high on peyote and didn't remember what he saw until his memory was sparked by the HBO film on the Pleasant Valley Two that came out some years after this happened. As his memory returned in full, he went into a depression for more than a year. He had to be hospitalized. After he recovered, he sought legal help. He wanted to go to the prosecutors and tell his story. After thoroughly questioning him and going over the records and transcripts, I told him I didn't think anyone would believe him. He felt guilty about not remembering, and believed it was his fault Dyme was convicted. He wanted to start a movement to get Dyme and the other man out of prison.

"I pointed out there were plenty of celebrities trying to help Dyme. I asked what he thought he could do that they could not. He'd thought of a plan and wanted me to help him implement it."

"Plan?" Brass worked to keep from rolling his eyes at this story.

"My client wanted to get the big fundamentalist churches involved by focusing on injustice in the legal system using films such as the one HBO did on the P.V. Two. He wanted me to approach several of them and pitch his idea. The churches would sponsor music festivals, get the proceeds from the vendors, the films would be free to the public. The idea was to generate interest among preachers and their congregations and then start up a grassroots campaign about injustice, not the P.V. Two. They were too polarizing. Once the injustice cause took hold, then a specific case would be introduced and that would be the P.V. Two.

"His idea gave me one that was less involved. There was an upcoming film festival in New York. The same HBO documentary was on the schedule. I invited Lauren to go with me to the festival. We saw the film and discussed it in detail. I made the remark that some bright con artist was going to look at the film and see the P.V Two as a meal ticket. They already had the celebrities, but Dyme needed a woman to humanize him. That was all I said and, as I knew she would, Lauren came up with the idea of writing him, and you know the story from there."

"Why would this client of yours need a lawyer?"

"Lawyers are often used as an interface. You know that. Take real estate, for example. If I wanted to buy your property and it wasn't for sale, I would hire a lawyer to contact you instead of doing so myself or getting a real estate agent. I could maintain my privacy."

"Why you?"

"I didn't ask. Probably because I own my own practice and work alone, and I have name recognition. I come from a big family of prominent lawyers in Louisiana."

"How old is your client?"

"Not relevant."

Brass allowed his eyes to travel around the kitchen, giving him time to let the pieces of what he'd heard fall into place. "MB. This is far-fetched. A man walks into a lawyer's office, tells her he believes that a famous convict did not commit the crime he is serving time for. He feels guilty for not going to the authorities when it happened, but he forgot what he saw, and years later he remembered. He asks the lawyer to help get the convict out of prison. The lawyer has a woman friend who is a grifter. She marries the convict, sets up a nonprofit to milk the donations and public sympathy, the con gets released. The con artist accuses the ex-convict of assault because he is sleeping with her best friend. The lawyer goes to the detective on the case, tells him the crazy story, tries to persuade him to not take the assault charges seriously so that her client won't get depressed again if the ex-con goes back to prison. Have I got that right?"

"Let me point out that this story is no more far-fetched than some of the episodes you write for your television crime shows. Think about it, Brass. Lauren made money. Dyme got out. My client doesn't feel guilty any longer. I made my attorney's fees. And I bet I will see some form of this on a future episode. I'd call that synergy, wouldn't you?"

"You don't care if Dyme is innocent or guilty. You only care about your client and his tendency toward guilt and depression. Right?"

"Exactly. Lauren's behavior threatens my client. I tried to reason with her without revealing my role, but she is on a mission."

"In the beginning you made the remark that I 'think' I know a great deal about Dawn because I've gotten into her secure site. Explain that."

"The journals, or what looks like journals, are a mixture of fact and fiction, written to throw out a bunch of red herrings if someone reads them. To know what is true, you would need to fact-check the whole thing."

"What about you, MB? Are you an actor like Dawn, playing the role of a female Bond, flying in here in a helicopter? What makes you think I've bought a word of your story, entertaining as it may be?"

MB handed Brass her business card. "You can start here."

Brass laid the card on the oak table. He stood and turned to leave the kitchen. He hurried, taking the steps two at a time, to his writing studio where he made a call to his partner to check out Bienville. He gazed at his view. He felt compromised by her unexpected arrival on his property. She'd disrespected his privacy, that disturbed him as much as her ease of finding where he lived and showing up like she had a right to be there. This pushy lawyer attracted and repelled him. One part of him was tempted to make sure Dyme went to prison to spite her. The better half of him said he would probably do the same thing if their places were reversed. Brass wanted justice, real justice, for everyone involved. When he returned to the kitchen, MB was texting. He noticed she had refilled her glass of tea. Apparently, she was planning on staying awhile.

"Who has the Calder?" said Brass.

"I don't know."

"Where is it?" Brass was in cop mode.

"Lauren asked me to ship something for her to Fayetteville, North Carolina. Fort Bragg Mini-Storage. It was a long narrow box. Maybe that's what you are looking for. She didn't say what it was, and I didn't look inside. It was sealed."

That was a test question. After going back and searching the shed, Brass found evidence that something had been recently boxed up. He found a set of boot prints, belonging either to a tall woman or a small man. He followed the prints to the overflow lot at the old Y building. A postal shop was in the shopping center nearby and he checked there and they showed him the shipping information.

"Who vandalized Horton's house?"

"I don't know. Look. I know you are checking me out. What you can't check is the story I've told you. It really isn't relevant when it comes down to it. Sabbath Dyme didn't assault Lauren, and it would be unjust to charge him. Lauren is an actress. Dawn is a character. She is like a person with multiple personalities except she changes them at will. I know her. She will persist and push and lie to get her way. Her wrists show the signs of being twisted and with her fair skin, the bruises stand out nicely in a photo. If the pictures do show she wasn't pushed, she will say she dove to save her life because he had grabbed her, twisted her to the ground, and she feared he would throw her off the deck.

"There are plenty of people around here who think Dyme's Alford plea stinks and resent the money Dyme's made since he's been out. Lauren has flipped sides and will scoop those Dyme haters up and use them. She will rally them and she will push the LRPD into arresting him. This whole mess is political for your department. If this had been Jane Jones accusing her husband of pushing her over a deck this would be just another domestic dispute. Here, look at this. It came up on YouTube this morning."

MB handed Brass her iPhone and watched Dawn's performance. It started with a close-up of purple bruises on white skin, backing off to a full face shot of Dawn looking worn out.

"The police won't help me. I'm in danger and you may be too. Sabbath Dyme attacked me and tried to drown me. I believed in him, fought for him, and this is how he repaid me."

MB said, "Here is Twitter. Scroll through it and you will get a good idea of the feelings out there. It looks to me like there is plenty of sympathy for her and anger at the police for not letting the public know Dyme was living in Little Rock."

Brass hadn't seen the YouTube video but he had kept up with Dawn's blog and Twitter. He didn't like what he was seeing. Dawn Daniels was running the show. Incredible.

Brass pulled up LenneVeeTruthPortal. "I've been following this blog for a couple of years. Its focus is primarily on law enforcement and the judicial system, the way they handle crimes against women. A few times it posted information I thought only detectives should have. Lenne Vee is taking the stand that Dyme didn't assault his wife and the police are hiding evidence that would prove it. Since Dawn Daniels moved to Little Rock and revved up the crusade to free the Pleasant Valley Two, Vee has written about Daniels and her fund-raising, but it hasn't dominated the blog.

"Look at LenneVeeTruthPortal this morning." Brass turned his iPad toward MB.

The blog read:

The cops are hiding important information from us. What else is new? Go to my Facebook and take a look at Dawn Daniels

performing a near perfect back dive off Connie Horton's deck. It is not Photoshop. I sent the shot to the *Arkansas Democrat-Gazette*. If that rag is interested in the truth, the editors will verify the authenticity and run the pictures on their front page. Is Sabbath Dyme being treated fairly by the LRPD and the press?
He is in limbo. Charge him or state there is no evidence of assault.
It looks like Dawn Daniels not the LRPD is running the show.

MB looked up from the screen. "Lauren said the Blue girl took photos of her. She could have sent them to the blogger. Would someone in your department do that?"

Brass said, "I've wondered if Vee is a female cop, one still young and idealistic, but not at our station, somewhere else in the state. Vee could be a group of young women, maybe college girls, pretending to be one person. He or she or they are very clever and resourceful. Go back and read some of the earlier stuff. Even you might be impressed. I wouldn't put it past the Blue kid to have sent the pictures. She is very smart and has a streak of the troublemaker in her."

Brass's cell vibrated. He stood up and walked into the saloon, as he still thought of the room although there were no more animal heads or fish bodies lining the walls.

Brass rolled the cue ball against the sides of the pool table and listened to what his partner had learned about MB. She came from a prominent New Orleans family, never married, highly respected in her field of environmental law, gave away a generous amount of pro bono hours, a world class poker player, a pilot certified in three types of aircraft, graduated second in her law class, and turned down offers with three of the largest environmental firms in the country to open her own practice. He wanted something personal but that would take more digging. He walked out of the saloon.

"Morel Baptiste Bienville," Brass said as she turned from the refrigerator holding the pitcher of tea. "Let's talk."

Chapter 21

Looking for the Calder - May 24, 2013

B rass traveled to Fort Bragg to accompany the officers who searched the storage unit for the Calder. He saw himself bringing the mobile back to Little Rock and then enjoying the pleasure of arresting Dawn Daniels.

The space was an odd combination of workshop and storage. To the left of the entrance was a wooden workbench with tools hanging according to use and size on the Peg-Board over it. Stainless shelving lined the side walls. It reminded Brass of the back room of a gift shop, the way the items were catalogued and stored in transparent containers or protective wrappings. In a rack against the back wall were framed pieces of artwork, oil paintings, acrylic, photographs in protective wrappings. The box containing the Calder lay on the workbench along with the paperwork showing when it was shipped and who signed for it when it arrived.

Brass opened a drawer and found a box cutter. He carefully sliced through the packing tape and folded back the thick cardboard. Three layers of bubble wrap covered the top of the object. When his fingers touched the plastic protective barrier he had a bad feeling about what he was going to find. There had been no evidence of bubble wrap in the shed. He'd found packing peanuts and there were none in this box.

It was with this on his mind that he removed the plastic to see three Japanese woodblocks, matted and framed as a unit, looking back at him as though it were Dawn Daniels herself calling him an idiot. The Calder wasn't at Fort Bragg.

"That fucking liar," said Brass under his breath.

"This isn't what you were looking for?" one of the officers asked, and it was all Brass could do to keep his reaction cool.

"Look through the rest of this place for another box this size, although I doubt you'll find it."

Brass documented the search and the contents of the box. He then called a small charter company for a flight to New Orleans, at his personal expense.

MB was still in her office when her assistant knocked on the door. MB called, "Come on in, Jimmy."

Jimmy slipped in, and closed it behind him. "Oh my god. There is this super hot guy out there to see you. He isn't a client. He says it is personal and he wants to surprise you. Have you been seeing someone and not telling? Naughty."

MB touched a button on her desk and the camera image in the reception area came up on the screen. Brass. He didn't look happy, pacing back and forth.

"Jimmy, that is a police detective. He's working on the case in Little Rock, the one I've told you about."

"Well, he is hot. Yum." Jimmy wore dark blue Brooks Brothers slacks, a long sleeved starched light blue shirt, and a yellow and blue patterned silk tie from Hermes. The clothes hid a body made lean, hard, and flexible from years of martial arts training. He wore his red hair cut short and that made his baby face look even more boyish.

"Should I send him in or make him wait? I say make him wait. I love the smooth yet rugged type."

MB looked at her watch. "Tell him I will be out in a few minutes. Put him in the conference room. Give him a glass of ice and a sparkling water."

Jimmy, probably the best paralegal in the state, had worked for MB since she started her practice. He'd been with the same domestic partner for ten years, a cosmetic surgeon, but Jimmy's inner flirt was never satisfied. What did satisfy him was the complimentary little nips and tucks, laser re-surfacing, and freebie pharmaceutical grade cosmetics to keep his skin smooth and creamy. Jimmy had worked for one of MB's uncles and when he retired, MB inherited him. Next to Joe, and Augustus, he was the best man in her life.

On his bumpy flight to New Orleans, Brass had examined every angle on the Calder theft, trying to assess what all the pieces meant. What he did know or thought he knew was that MB was Dawn's partner in the crime. He went over what he suspected. Dawn had stolen the Calder and had vandalized the place to create a diversion. Like a good magician, she had MB draw attention away from the box that contained the mobile to a decoy box. MB had picked up the decoy from the shed and shipped it. MB had claimed she didn't know about the vandalism or what the box contained. He didn't believe her.

When he had asked MB why she shipped the box instead of taking it with her, she said Dawn wanted it in her Fort Bragg storage unit and they were going to New Orleans. MB told him that Dawn had asked her to come to Little Rock as moral support because she was going to confront Dyme about his affair with the student. Dawn planned to leave him and Delphi Pond. She wanted to get some personal items from the house but he had the car and she couldn't load her things up before she confronted him. She didn't know how he would react and worried she would not be able to return to get her things. Dawn had said the neighbors were nosey, and she didn't want them to see anyone coming to the house carting off boxes. Dawn told her to take the path behind the house to avoid them. MB had said she thought there would be more than one box but there was not.

Brass was hung up on whether MB had picked up more than one box. She admitted shipping one. Had she taken others with her? When he asked MB why Dawn had not left Little Rock with her, MB had said it was a last minute change of plan on Dawn's part. She wanted to see that Dyme was charged with assault. Brass thought it was all so clear now. Dawn had stayed to create the assault diversion so that MB could get the Calder out of town. Brass did not trust MB Bienville.

Brass could see now how MB had worked him. She could have lied about the shipment and the storage unit when he asked her about it earlier in the investigation, but she had told the truth. She might have figured Brass knew about the shipment already, and it was a test question, or she wanted to send him on a false trail and divert his attention from the theft. He began to wonder about the relationship between Dawn and MB, their friendship—or were they friends at all? What did a top tier attorney see in a grifter? They'd known each other a long time, so MB had said, yet what was their friendship built on? What or who would be important enough for MB to choose not to support Dawn on her assault charge against Dyme? Who or what was more important to MB than her old friend Dawn? He was having a hard time believing the mystery client story she had told him.

Brass tried to play his own cross-examiner and asked himself why he was so convinced that Dawn had vandalized the property and stolen the Calder with MB's help. Brass believed the two things went hand in hand. Like most cops, he shied away from coincidence although he did not dismiss it. There was such a thing as coincidence and maybe Dawn had not vandalized the house. Maybe she simply took advantage of the chaos it created to steal the Calder. That was not unlike what MB's mystery client had claimed: Dyme came across the already dead boys and took advantage of the crime to perform one of his sick rituals. Who would have a reason to tear up the Horton place just for the pleasure of destroying it or to cause Connie Horton pain?

Brass considered the possibility that a professional art thief planned the vandalism and the theft. It was not an uncommon thing to do, create a diversion. The vandalism also made it hard to collect evidence. Then he remembered that had been his first impression, thieves after the Calder, the vandalism to cover the evidence. Dawn could have done the same thing. She was capable. He admitted to himself he was letting the drama of Delphi Pond cloud his judgment and that showed him maybe his days as a cop were about over. He would think on that later.

Brass was going over these events again in his mind while he waited for MB. When he turned from the view of the river to face her as she walked in the room, his instinct was to believe that she was an honest person, but his logical mind told him she was devious.

MB strode into the conference room looking impatient and utterly bereft of the Southern charm he associated with her. She'd been in court most of the day and still wore her dark red suit with a crisp white shirt, open two buttons from the collar. Her jewelry was simple, one large black pearl at her throat. Her hair was pulled back in a French braid knotted at the nape of her neck. She wore no makeup except for base, a little mascara, and a pair of white pearl studs in her ears.

"What is wrong?" MB didn't see any point in attempting the hospitality thing. Today, Brass looked like one of the many cops she'd dealt with over the years. He was on the offensive. It could be seen in the set of his jaw, the hard look in his eyes, the position of his legs, a little far apart as if to steady himself against a blow.

"I think you know." Brass thought he could tell by looking at her she didn't but he wasn't sure, so he bluffed. He realized for the first time, he could not read her. His digging showed she was a near genius poker player and that was probably why.

MB went to a credenza that stood beneath a Carroll Cloar painting titled *New Born Calf*. She removed the bottle of Angostura 1824, two glasses, put a cube of ice in each, and poured the rum. She handed Brass a glass without asking him if he wanted a drink.

"I can't claim to be on duty when I'm not in my own territory, so what the hell." Brass was either looking at a real good liar or an innocent bystander. He was determined that he would have her pinned down before he left her fancy office.

"Have a seat and let's talk it out. Then you can get on with your life and so can I." MB indicated the conference table. They sat across from each other. She faced the bend in the river while he looked at the far wall. A beveled mirror ran the length of it so he found he was looking back at himself.

"I went to the storage unit this morning. I want *you* to see the results of my search." He pulled out his iPhone and ran the video. He watched MB as she looked at the little screen.

"What do you make of what's in the box?" Brass watched her face for tells as she answered.

"Those are rare Japanese double image woodblocks by Yoshiku created around 1850."

"I can see they are woodblocks. What I am asking is what are they doing in the box?"

MB gave him a stare. "Detective, how would I know that answer?"

"MB. Do you know anything at all about the woodblocks that would help me understand why they were important enough for Dawn to pack them up and have you ship on the day the house was vandalized?"

"I can only tell you what I know, not what's in Lauren's mind. When Lauren rented an apartment from me fifteen years ago, she brought those with her. It was the only personal item in the place except her clothing and jewelry. I think they belonged to her grandmother."

Brass followed up. "What did you think was in the box, considering its shape?"

"I didn't know what it contained."

"Why would Dawn ask you go to the trouble of sneaking into the shed to take this box and ship it?" Brass asked.

"Her car wasn't at the house so she couldn't pack her things before her talk with Dyme, just like I said. She didn't want to leave it behind at Connie's. The Yoshiku woodblocks are sentimental. She has taken them with her to every place she has lived. A work of art needs caring for. These are valuable, and they are part of her family history. It is the family aspect not the financial value that is most important to her."

"You are telling me this is about sentimentality? I'm having a hard time with that one."

MB pushed back. "I saw where you live and I know the story, how you built that storage area for Manny's belongings that came along with his house, a man you didn't know, yet you did it because you felt the vibe, the importance of his things. I know you didn't say it that way, but why would a man like you keep the history of another man? I'm not saying it makes you weak, Brass. It makes you sensitive. You then, of all people, should understand why Dawn would ask me to help her keep her precious object safe. Are you accusing me of knowingly sending you on a wild goose chase?"

Brass shrugged. "Maybe I would have gone on it anyway. I went back to the shed after I learned about the theft. I found packing materials. I saw footprints. I knew something had been packed and someone had taken it from the shed. I assumed it was the Calder. I tracked the box down. Today, I went to the storage unit, as you can see."

"I do see and clearly. When you asked me about this matter the other day, you already had the answer. You were testing me. The downside of that, Brass, is you still don't know if I lied to you or not."

Brass didn't respond. It had been a statement not a question.

MB attempted to lighten the mood. "I don't blame you. Who in their right mind would trust a Southern woman?"

"You tell me she had the woodblocks in New Orleans. You could be covering for her."

"Wait here." MB left the room and came back with an antique hat box. "My memory box," she explained as she dug through the clippings, cards, and snapshots, that had been randomly tossed inside over many years. "Here. What do you see?" She handed Brass a photograph of her and Lauren, much younger, standing with a dark haired man. In the background were the woodblocks, mounted together in a single wooden frame, just as Brass had found them. Another photo, a different room, the two of them looking a little older, the same framed work in the background.

"This is your proof unless you think I've created a Photoshop fake just for you. Take it to your lab. These woodblocks are important to Lauren as part of her family history."

"Who is the man in the picture?"

"Not pertinent to your investigation."

"Did he have a relationship with Dawn?"

"Brass! You are reaching and that is death for a cop."

"Did you pick up two boxes of the same shape and take one of them back with you and mail the other one?"

"I did not pick up two boxes. I don't have corroboration on that fact except from Lauren. If you think I am telling a lie then you think I am a thief. So prove it." MB showed nothing on her face. To her this was a game. She didn't have anything to hide or to find. That left her in the power position.

"Do you think Dawn is the vandal and the thief?" asked Brass. He hadn't tasted his drink. His fingers slowly rotated the glass on the wooden coaster. The motion calmed him like prayer beads would soothe a person who believed in them.

MB folded her hands and set them on the walnut table. "I think Dawn is capable of taking advantage of a situation such as finding the place torn up and then taking the Calder or doing both of those things. She is also enough of a persuader to inspire Beau to do that work for her. If Beau thought Connie was having sex with Dyme under Dawn's nose, it would remind him of what he went through. He may have decided it was time to punish Connie because he had not in the past. Have you considered that the vandal and the thief is Beau?"

Brass said, "He's not off my list and neither are you. Frankly, I can also see this as the work of a pro. From what I know about Connie, any thief with internet access could have learned about her collection. I am certain the chief is not going to be happy about what I didn't find to-day. I can't see the department trying to track down an art thief. Maybe Horton's insurance company will do that."

Brass lifted the glass and took a deep drink. "That's good." He took his cell out of his back pocket and called his partner. "Have a talk with Beau Bowen and put the pressure on him."

MB said, "Brass, you're stuck on thinking Dawn and I stole the Calder. Maybe you should open your mind a little. The day is over. Take a break. You are in New Orleans." She called Jimmy in. "Would you make a reservation for two at—"

MB looked at Brass. "Gumbo or fish. Antoine's, run by the same family since the Civil War, or GW Fins? Their menu is built around fish flown in daily. Both have great desserts and atmosphere. Tourists love them. If you ever come back this way, I will take you where the locals eat, but tonight, I think you need the Quarter. The old or the new? You choose."

Brass hesitated.

"I'm into the lobster dumplings at Fins. That's where I would go," Jimmy suggested.

MB said, "Okay. Fins. That works for me. Make it for eight if you don't mind, Jimmy, then go on home. It's been a long day."

Jimmy sighed. "Thank you, mistress." He gave a little bow.

MB stood, took off her jacket, and hung it in the closet. Then she walked to a door next to the bar and opened it, she shut the door behind her and came out a few minutes later wearing a pair of black Lululemon capri pants, a vertical striped black and white loose fitting top, and a pair of FitFlops. She'd shaken out the knotted braid and let her long hair hang free. She refreshed her drink and indicated Brass follow her into the private sitting area next to her office.

MB sat in a black leather Barcelona chair and Brass took the twin across the low lacquer oriental table from her. MB didn't like her furni-ture to match. Perhaps that was the Creole in her and an oriental touch was the perfect complement to the steel and leather of the chair. MB didn't envy her married friends who had to negotiate the type of furni-ture or the color of the walls with their spouses.

"I haven't heard from Dawn since I left Little Rock. I'm feeling a little bit left out. What's she up to? I bet you know."

"She's using all the social media to keep the focus on the assault. You probably know that."

"I was wondering if you would be so kind as to share with me what the world doesn't know."

Still all business, Brass said, "We are investigating all aspects of the case. I can't get into any of it with you. She's staying in her old room at Missy McShane's place. Other than that, there's nothing I can say."

MB leaned toward Brass and touched his hand with her index finger. Her nails were manicured and polished with clear gloss. "I think your palm needs reading, a natal chart should be done to understand your past, a tarot card reading for your future, and a session with a psychic to give you access to the unknown, all of which can be supplied to you right here in New Orleans this evening. Should I ask Jimmy to make a few calls before he leaves?"

"Maybe that is exactly what I need to free me from the curse of Delphi Pond." The aged rum was beginning to work its magic on the detective.

Chapter 22

Ha'ina la ami ana ka puana - May 29, 2013

After five days hiding in the Mann on Main loft, Sabbath Dyme was going stir crazy. He didn't feel free at all, no matter how big the apartment. He wanted to go to the River Market and walk around, go to the Clinton library, walk across the pedestrian bridge to North Little Rock, maybe have lunch at the Starving Artist Cafe. He needed to feel some normalcy, although he didn't know if he would recognize that if he saw it. He didn't want to stand out anymore.

On his first day, Dyme had given his bodyguard a couple of hundreds and asked him to go find something mainstream Little Rock for him to wear. The bodyguard came back with jeans, a plaid cowboy shirt, a pair of running shoes, a ball cap with a razorback on the front, and a pair of Ray-Ban Aviators. Dyme didn't put on the clothes. He laid on the sofa and turned on the television without the sound.

Here he was in this fancy loft with every kind of liquor and a gigantic television. All he wanted was a good book to read. If he had a Kindle he could download some of his favorite writers but Dyme preferred hard books; the light of the Kindle hurt his eyes. He used his iPhone and looked up bookstores in the area. There was a used book depot just a few blocks away. They even had a coffee shop. He liked the looks of it and planned to walk down there but hadn't yet managed it. His bodyguard had said something about it being a good idea to blend

in and not look like Dracula. Dyme resented the crack even as he eyed
the new clothes. Leave or not leave the loft? Dyme couldn't decide as
his eyes traveled over the books lining the shelves. They were the genre
of books men in prison read: thrillers, crime, adventure, action, for-
mula books. His eye fell on a title that compelled him enough to get up
and take the book from the shelf. *Never Go Back* was the last in a series
about a former military cop called Jack Reacher. The entire series was
on the shelf, lined up in order, as was the Clive Clusser series about
the NUMA files, James Patterson, Douglas Preston and Lincoln Child,
and other popular writers who wrote about crime and adventure. He
picked up the first in the Reacher series and laid back down on the sofa.
He read it and went on to number two, three, four, until he finished all
of them.

What surprised Dyme after getting into the Reacher books was his
fascination with the fictional character's way of life. He had left the
military, walked out on his life, and taken to the road. He lived simply,
didn't own a house or a car, or even have a current driver's license, yet
he got by. He hitchhiked, walked, or took a bus wherever he went. The
only personal items he carried with him were an ATM card, an ex-
pired passport for ID, a fold up toothbrush, and the clothes on his back.
When the clothes were dirty, he went to a discount store and bought a
new shirt and pants and threw the old ones in the trash on his way out
the door. Reacher was a free man who didn't answer to anyone. Dyme
wanted that for himself.

Dyme looked at the new clothes his bodyguard had bought for him
four or five days earlier. He couldn't remember. He didn't even know
the day of the week. He held the plaid cowboy shirt up to his chest,
looked in the mirror, and then put the shirt on over his black T. The
long sleeves covered his arms that were heavily tattooed with over
forty different images. A collection of totems, Anna Blue had called
them. The jeans were a little big but the belt took care of that. His new
running shoes fit perfectly. He pulled the ball cap down low on his
forehead and put on the Ray-Bans. He looked in his wallet, counted his
money, and made sure his driver's license was still there. He left the loft
without locking the door. He told his bodyguard he wanted to be alone.
The bodyguard, who had strong opinions about Dyme, had no problem
sending him off into a hostile world. Dyme walked across the street to
the Sports Page, a restaurant with a bar in the back.

For a short time it had been a jazz club called Porter's, named after a local jazz piano player. Bar patrons walked through the restaurant to get to the bar. The history of the club was in the black and white photographs still hanging on the walls.

Dyme thought he looked like a contractor, what with the blue jeans and the plaid. His black T underneath gave his chest a little bulk. There was plenty of construction going on downtown. No one looked up as he walked in and took a stool at the bar in the back. Even though it was noon, not too many people were in the place. The bar was pleasantly dark and cool inside. He didn't need his sunglasses but he kept them on anyway.

Dyme sat with his back to the door and kept an eye on the entrance by looking into the mirror behind the bar. The male bartender wore tight black jeans, a tight black V-neck T that showed off his body builder's muscles. The servers wore black, so did the host, and Dyme would have been in black himself if he hadn't chosen to wear this disguise. Now he felt like he stood out. In black he would have blended. He wouldn't have looked like Dracula at all. That comment still chapped his ass.

In contrast to his hard body, the barman's face was almost pretty, with his curly hair, full lips, easy smile, and light blue eyes.

Dyme sat down and ordered a Red Stripe.

The bartender said, "You look like you need beans more than beer. The devil haunts a hungry man."

"What?" Dyme felt his torso pull back.

"I've been listening to Kristofferson." He grinned, it was a wide smile showing white teeth. He motioned to the speakers and then Dyme heard the country western coming softly out of them, the sound seeming to hover around the bar, not reaching the restaurant's tables.

"I don't know the song." His lack of knowledge here made Dyme feel diminished, emotionally and physically. He wondered if it showed. His eyes fell on his hands, "do nothing hands" that were soft, white, and thin with a single symbol tattooed on each first knuckle. The bartender's hands were strong and beefy, like his arms and shoulders. Strong, he thought, like Dawn's hands were, but he hadn't seen or felt the strength in them until she punched him in the chest, nearly knocking him off his feet.

"We don't have Stripe. We have a local beer on draft. Want to give it a try?"

"Sure." Dyme wasn't in the mood to make decisions. Then he realized he was out of practice. If Dawn didn't make his decisions for him it was his lawyers or Connie or the prison officials. Dyme kept his eyes on the mirror behind the bar, looking at customers make their way in. He didn't like to keep his back to a room but the mirror made him feel safer about it. When the bartender set the cold mug down, Dyme jumped.

"Looks like you might need something a little stronger to take the edge off those nerves. On the house." He reached back, took a bottle of silver Patron off the top shelf, and poured Dyme a shot. The tequila had the opposite effect. It set his nerves further on edge. Dawn and Connie's ritualistic drink, beer and tequila. Dyme looked around for a table. The barman spooked him. He thought he might order something to eat when the man handed him a menu.

"I can take your order and serve you here."

"Are you reading my mind?"

"Like I said, you look like a hungry man."

Dyme was hungry but he didn't know for what. It wasn't food. Maybe peace. Maybe true freedom. His mind drifted back to that morning of coffee and biscotti with Anna Blue and her mother. Not many days went by that he didn't think of that visit, how after he left them, he cut his leather duster to shreds with a box cutter and threw the pieces into the pond.

That morning he had told Anna Blue and her mother that Dawn had advised him that he didn't need to have in-depth knowledge of anything he read, he only needed just enough to throw out a few catchy phrases, enough to sound educated. He understood what Dawn meant, create an illusion, but he was more than Dawn's creation. He had been hungry for the knowledge and had taught himself what he thought the great philosophers had to say. They kept him sane. Yet he had let Anna and her mother think he was a shallow reader and a shallow man.

He thought about his cell on death row and how it had given him time to develop his artistic side. He had taught himself to draw and created album covers for several heavy metal rock bands. His drawings had been part of a major show in New York. He now wondered if he had been part of that show not because his work was great but because he was an oddity, a freak, a convict set free, a celebrity who would attract more people to the show. A Dancing Bear. He had two self-published memoirs that hadn't sold very well, but it meant he was called an author. Now he wished he'd gotten a real publisher. He had not wasted the eighteen years in prison, he had taught himself much and had set himself up for his current job, making money just being Sabbath Dyme and going around talking about it.

He also regretted telling Anna Blue that he did not write the Dyme Letters. She and her mother saw him as a fraud because of it. When the idea about the Dyme Letters had come up, Sabbath had been excited about communicating directly with his supporters. Then he saw the need in Beau to express his understanding of Sabbath's situation and he had backed away to let Beau do what he did so well. A movement in the mirror caught his attention and brought him into the present.

In the mirror he saw the door open and his bodyguard come in and take a table for two near the door. Dyme guessed he had finally decided to take his job seriously and do what he was paid to do. The wall on the other side of the restaurant was lined with posters of the jazz greats: Dizzy Gillespie, Bill Evans, Miles Davis, and so on, including Art Porter, the deceased piano man. He listened to the conversations around him and figured most people worked in the area. A few were tourists in town for the Riverfest.

A woman, a tall blonde dressed in high heels, tight jeans, and a form fitting top that showed off her small waist, walked in alone and sat at the bar a few stools over from him. She ordered a Don Julio 70, neat. She sat there looking like she was used to being alone.

Dyme picked up the menu and looked it over. He felt his body needed fuel. Maybe the classic cheeseburger. Maybe the guacamole, no too cold. He needed something heavy and warm. He was thinking these things when he saw the tall man come into the restaurant and walk toward the bar. His features seemed familiar. He wore a white, long sleeved shirt tucked into jeans, and a worn leather belt with a large buckle. His broad shoulders were wide and strong and stretched the fabric of the cotton shirt, his legs were strong too, he moved like an athlete. Dyme had a flashback to one of the guards at Varner and he felt a little chill run up his legs, up his spine, and across the back of his neck.

When the bartender asked if he'd like another beer and Patron, Dyme moved his eyes off the mirror to look at him. When Dyme looked back into the mirror he saw that his bodyguard was gone. Dyme felt a nervousness stir in his gut. In Varner, guards were feared, out in the free world Sabbath depended on them. He relied on lawyers, guards, women, celebrities, but not one bit on himself, and for the first time since he got out, he admitted to himself he was ashamed of his dependence on all of them.

Dyme jumped when he felt a hand on his shoulder. The tall man then spoke to him. "Remember me? Bill Brass, LRPD." Brass took the stool next to his.

The bartender said, "You look like a Duvel man to me."

Brass nodded in agreement and Dyme watched as he soft poured the Belgium ale. Brass waited until the head settled before he sipped. He saw Dyme check the mirror again.

He said, "He won't be back. You're on your own."

"What?"

"I said he is gone. No more guard. You are free to go on with your life, such as it is. You are not going to be charged with assault."

"Dawn isn't mad at me anymore?"

Brass was in the process of lifting the glass but stopped. He looked at Dyme letting his eyes move up and down the man. "I don't think I've met a bigger fool than you, Dyme."

The bartender waited until Brass stopped speaking then he handed Dyme an envelope. "The seating host asked me to give you this."

Dyme looked at the envelope. Attached to it was a paper clip. The bartender said, "There was a twenty attached. The host kept the cash."

"Looks like you've got mail, Dyme." Brass noticed a little tremor in Dyme's hand as he took the envelope.

"You mean you've come here to tell me this nightmare is over?" Dyme's voice sounded hopeful even to him.

"I won't even speculate about what you mean by 'over.' " Brass spoke in a flat tone.

Over, Brass thought. It was over as far as he was concerned. That debacle in North Carolina embarrassed him. He should have let the locals handle it but instead he went over there himself, spending department funds, making a point, putting himself out there for criticism from other detectives when nothing came of it.

Brass couldn't think of another day in his career like today, when the pieces of a case fell neatly into place one right after the other. He didn't buy it but the convenience of it all suited the department and that was the only thing that mattered in police work it seemed, covering the department's ass. Maybe it was time for him to move on. He didn't need the work. He enjoyed it. It kept his mind sharp for his writing and a detective's badge opened doors.

The first piece had dropped in place when Dawn Daniels's attorney called first thing this morning and asked him to come by his office. Brass went immediately. Daniels was there. They had prepared an affidavit stating she had suffered "misattribution of memory due to trauma." Brass knew about misattribution. He'd heard that term used in court when cases went to trial. According to Daniels's statement, after a few sessions with a therapist her memory had been restored, and she remembered the actual event. Dyme did not assault or push her. She fell over the rail. It was an accident. Brass wanted to question her about the photo showing the dive. He wanted to make her admit she deliberately went into the water, but he didn't pursue it. The chief would not like that. So he let it go.

There were dozens of questions Brass wanted to ask but none of them had anything to do with the case. He wanted to know if Horton's pre-Columbian pottery collection was heavily peppered with reproductions. He thought that it was. Was the Matisse sketch of Mother and Child authentic? He didn't think so. There were several pieces he had photographed in Dawn's storage unit, such as the Matisse, that matched items in the Horton collection.

Brass had a partial list of the collection along with photographs of the pieces the Arkansas Arts Center had displayed before Horton met Daniels. Brass suspected that during the time they lived together, the more valuable pieces were reproduced and swapped for the originals. He couldn't prove it without gaining entrance to the storage unit again and that was not going to happen. Even if he got a warrant, which was impossible without a very good reason. He knew because he had tried to obtain one on probable cause. Anyway, he suspected everything that had been in the unit was already gone.

There was so much about the case that wasn't explained. Instead of trying to solve it on his own, which he would have to do since the case was now closed, he figured he could make better use of what he knew and suspected as material for his screenplays or maybe challenge himself and write a novel about it.

Less than two hours after he left Daniels and her attorney, as he was finishing up his final report, he received a call from Connie Horton. The second piece fell in place. Federal Express had delivered a package to her that morning. It contained the Calder mobile. Brass asked if he could stop by and inspect it, but she said that wasn't necessary. When he inquired if she was going to have it authenticated to confirm it was the original, she said that unlike him, she could recognize a fake. This was her Calder, an original, she assured him. When he questioned her about the container it arrived in and asked to examine it, she refused that also. Her property had been returned and she didn't want any more to do with the police. She asked him to close the case or whatever it took for him to never return to her house and slammed down the phone.

Brass didn't tell her that Daniels had sent all of AFJ's financial information to the newspapers, the attorney general, to him, every known interested party. Connie Horton was going to be tied up in audits, questioned by AFJ supporters, and speculated about in the media for a long time. He wondered what LenneVeeTruthPortal would have to say about all of this.

Brass looked over at Dyme, the last piece of the puzzle. The unopened envelope was still in his hand, and Dyme was staring at it like he thought it was going to speak.

The padded envelope was light. He examined the outside of it as if it would give a clue to the contents. He pulled back the flap and found a typed letter and a debit card inside. The letter read:

> *I hope you have asked yourself this question: If the devil came to me again and said, "I promise you fame if you will spend eighteen years of your life behind bars." Would I do it again?*
>
> *As of today, what has fame brought you other than having yourself defined in Wikipedia, or searched for in Google, or described by bloggers, or fleeting friendships with celebrities,*

or temporary appearances at book signings and art shows? Is your life today as big as you thought it was meant to be?

We are all hurtling through space, wondering how we got here, forgetting the initial collision of events responsible for us all. Quirks of fate, such as finding two dead boys or a woman falling into a pond, often decide our future.

In this envelope, I am giving you the means to start a new life, one determined by you, one that you own, not the life of the Dancing Bear that you are today.

Ha'ina la ami ana ka puana

"What the hell?" Dyme looked in the direction of Brass. He wasn't on the stool any longer, neither was the tall blond woman a few seats over, or the bartender with the speckled blue eyes. Dyme felt alone.

He took his iPhone out and Googled the foreign words. They were Hawaiian. *Ha'ina la ami ana ka puana* meant "the story is told."

Dyme let those words ramble around in his imagination, waiting for inspiration. He wanted the great thinkers from the beginning of time to send him a word or two. The only word that came to him was *Reacher.*

Dyme laid a hundred on the bar and walked through the restaurant and out the door where he stood on the sidewalk in the sunshine for several minutes.

He unbuttoned the plaid shirt, rolled it in a ball, and shoved it into the nearest sidewalk trash can along with his cell phone. Looking toward the north, he started walking. He crossed the Main Street bridge into North Little Rock, walked through the renovated business area called Argenta, and kept on walking. He had everything he needed, the clothes on his back, a debit card, money in his wallet. Well, almost everything, he needed a fold up toothbrush.

Dyme's soon-to-be-ex-wife was seated in a Cessna Citation Mustang while MB Bienville made the run up before takeoff. Augustus sat in the copilot's seat. He had a pilot's license too but was not trained in the Citation.

Lauren sat with her iPad on her lap, in the first passenger seat, making a reservation. She searched for houses to lease on the North Shore of Maui. The scuba diving wasn't too good in Hawaii, not like in Fiji or Australia or other places in the Pacific. There were no deep water wrecks like in the Philippines. Hawaiian reefs are shallow and the coral rudimentary, around Maui, Lanai, and Molokini. Diving there is excellent for the novice or for snorkeling. The water is warm, clear, and nonthreatening. For the diver looking for drop off diving to depths over two hundred meters, those islands aren't the place to go. Cozumel would be a better choice for that.

Lauren was interested in learning to kite board, and she wanted to stand-up paddle the North Shore of Maui and ride the big waves at Ho'okipa. The ocean restored her, and she needed a mending of her spirit after living a lie for so long. She'd rest until the next Worthy Cause presented itself.

Lauren read the relief on MB's face when she had told her that she decided to drop the assault accusation. Lauren had sent MB a copy of the affidavit and she approved of the way it was being handled. MB had said that now she could quit worrying about her. But Lauren didn't completely buy that. There was a little something off, but Lauren made the decision not to go there in her mind. The Sabbath Dyme Cause was now in the past.

Lauren would never tell MB about Gene, or the Calder theft, the re-production, the sale of the original which funded Dyme's new life and hers too with money left over. Lauren was headed to Hawaii. She didn't care what Sabbath Dyme was up to.

June 6, 2013

SABBATH DYME

This is my last communication with my supporters and my detractors. I am choosing a life that I can manage on my own. I am sure there will be sightings. Like with Elvis and Jim Morrison. I am tired of wearing my past like a skin. Tired of feeling indebted. Tired of being Sabbath Dyme and carrying around the baggage that goes with it. I am tired of being a Dancing Bear.

I chose the TruthPortal as my venue instead of my own website, or my publicist, my manager, my attorneys, my friends. LenneVeeTruthPortal hasn't judged me innocent or guilty. The Portal is neither a supporter nor a hater. The TruthPortal just is.

I threw my cell phone away and left behind every stitch of clothing I have collected since I got off death row. I own one pair of work boots, one pair of glasses, a pair of pants, a shirt, and will get a jacket when I need one. I am finally a free man.

Sabbath Dyme

About the Author

H. K. Finley is a graduate of the University of Arkansas at Little Rock. She holds an MA in public history, with an emphasis on research and writing. *The Worthy Cause* is her first novel.

She currently divides her time between Little Rock, where she was born and raised, and upcountry Maui.

www.ingramcontent.com/pod-product-compliance
Lightning Source LLC
Chambersburg PA
CBHW051511170626
46811CB00002B/752